Drak
The Cowboy an

CU00373512

She's full of life and made for adventure. He's built from family responsibilities and devotion to commitments.

The last thing Drake Presley needs is to be attracted to the lavender-eyed beauty with a teasing tongue and no sense of what responsibility means. She's a roamer built for leaving. Only problem—he can't stop thinking about her, and despite the fact that they rub each other the wrong way, she seems to have decided that it's her all-fired duty to loosen him up.

Free-spirited Maisy Love is determined to see all fifty states, traveling in her refurbished travel trailer as she cooks her way across the country. Focused on her internet show, On The Road with Maisy Love, she's found the perfect place for her next show, the Goodnight Café. The fact the place is full of handsome cowboys is an added bonus for her viewers.

Trouble is, she tangled with a skunk and a handsome cowboy with serious green eyes, and her world just turned upside down. A relationship is not part of her plans.

Too bad for her. Drake Presley is gorgeous, tempting, and despite smelling like a skunk, he draws her like a bee to honey water.

Fireworks like never before are shooting off this summer and it's not from the town celebration. Can these two opposites come to an agreement on the subject of love?

DRAKE:
THE COWBOY AND MAISY LOVE
Cowboys of Ransom Creek, Book Six

DEBRA
CLOPTON

Drake: The Cowboy and Maisy Love
Copyright © 2018 Debra Clopton Parks

CHAPTER ONE

Maisy Love's gut told her something was wrong, and her gut was usually right.

Driving her Jeep down the deserted country road, pulling her small travel trailer behind her, she hoped this time it was wrong. She was in the boonies, the middle of nowhere because she'd decided on the spur of the moment to detour. Yep, that same gut had said go for it and she had altered her course from her Texas Hill Country destination and taken a side trip down a stretch of road she'd not explored before. She was now skirting the hill country area very much off the beaten track.

Been here done this before, if it wasn't for her stinkin' gut churning now, she'd still be excited at the prospect of finding a few new diners appropriate for her food blog and live video channel. Sometimes the best places were discovered by accident. Or detours.

The Jeep jerked and made a weird noise. Her heart lurched in surprise and she pressed the brake and got the Jeep to the side of the road. Drat her gut, right again.

Breathing a sigh of relief that the wheels were not rolling any longer she put the Jeep in park and turned it off just as another weird noise came from somewhere beneath her or behind her. Was it the Jeep or the trailer?

She opened the door, jumped out and bent down to look under the Jeep and the travel trailer.

"Oh no," she gasped. There was a piece she was pretty sure wasn't supposed to dangle down under the trailer. This was not good.

Not good at all.

Still, on her knees, she looked down the deserted

road and ran through her options. She really only had one: call for help, because she certainly had no idea how to fix whatever it was that was wrong. Of course, traveling state to state, pulling her home behind her as she interviewed small-town café owners across the country for her internet show, On The Road with Maisy Love, exposed her to all sorts of new adventures. She loved her career. Though it was a one-woman show, she was able to support her travel habit with the income she made from ads and merchandise she sold in her Maisy Love store. It was a dream come true. She'd just recently sent an email with a video clip, taking a long shot at getting a spot on a cooking competition on the Food Network. The idea of actually competing against other foodies was a little nerve-racking but it would be great exposure.

And right now, though she was doing okay financially, some extra exposure to help bring in some extra money for emergency repairs like this was greatly needed. She pulled her phone from her pocket and made the road service call. Thankfully she'd paid the extra fee to AAA that enabled towing for a hundred miles or so and there just happened to be a small town called Ransom Creek not too far down the road.

While she waited for the tow truck, she pulled the small ranching town up on her phone app and was relieved to see that it sounded like a great place to check out while repairs were being made, if they had a mechanic. Another quick search showed that yes they had one but only one. They also showed a café for her to check out, the Goodnight Café. She loved the name and hoped the food and the owner lived up to the cute name. If so, Maisy may have just found her next show.

Forever the optimist she was smiling when the rust covered wrecker came to her rescue.

Drake Presley was a cowboy, *not* a skunk wrangler.

Still, here he stood, hidin' out on the back porch of the Goodnight Café in wait for a stinking polecat that had been showing up behind the café off and on for the last month. It was good at avoiding the cage traps but needed to be caught. It had almost sprayed Gert twice when she'd gone out to her storage building before she'd asked for help. And this morning she'd twisted her ankle running up the steps, getting away from the critter. Thankfully, she hadn't gotten sprayed, but she was going to be hurting for a few days.

He wasn't going to let her get hurt again. He was going to trap him a skunk and haul it off to the woods away from people.

Shifting his weight from one leg to the other as impatience welled within him, he peeked toward the shed, looking from his hiding place against the back wall of the diner's porch. He studied the shed and the surrounding vacant lots stretching out from it toward the old gas station, turned repair shop, that set down the road.

Nothing. His brows dipped. If ever there was a sneaky skunk, this was it. They'd set traps, and it had somehow managed to not enter the cage.

His phone buzzed in his pocket. He slipped it out and saw his brother, Brice's, name on the ID. "What?" he hissed in a barely audible sound.

"You sound weird."

"I'm standing here trying to surprise a skunk that's

probably going to shoot me with both his spray guns before I catch him. How do you think I'm supposed to sound?"

Brice chuckled. "Right, so, no luck?"

"Not yet," he growled, scanning the area. "Did you need something in particular?"

"Just checking on you. I went by the hospital and checked on Gert. She's going to be off her feet for a week or so."

"I was afraid of that."

"Do you need help? I'll bring reinforcements."

"Thanks, but I've got this."

There was a pause. "I've heard that before but it was worth a try."

When they were kids, after his mother died while in childbirth with their little sister, Lana, Drake had been the oldest and had instantly taken on the role as his dad's helper. And he'd always tried to handle everything himself. Those years had been hard, just from the loss of his mother and the horrible adjustments the family had had to make during that time. But he'd not helped matters sometimes because he'd taken his role so seriously. They all knew now that that had been his way of coping. But it hadn't been easy and he still, sometimes tried to take care of everything instead of asking for help.

"No need for both of us to possibly get sprayed—" he halted mid-sentence when he heard something. "Hey, gotta go. I think it's game time."

"Good luck and don't get sprayed…"

Drake hung up as his brother's chuckles rang from the phone.

Maisy walked from the repair shop toward the diner. Lenny, the mechanic told her it would take a few days to get her antique Jeep fixed. Then he'd told her where the diner was and suggested she go there for some lunch and figure things out. He'd told her about a nice bed-and-breakfast down the street from the diner and said that she should go there and get Sally Ann to set her up for a few days. Most people would be stressed about this news, but Maisy glanced around and felt optimistic about her whole adventure.

She could dig spending a few days here. Especially if the café was as good as he'd said. She wasn't sure how much trust to put in the little man's description of the food, not when he had looked as if he'd give a greasy burger a five-star rating, but considering this looked like maybe her only option, she was hoping every rave review he'd given the owner Gert Goodnight and her Goodnight Café was as deserving as he stated. She loved hitting the off-beaten track and finding fun new places; she had high hopes as she took the shortcut across the vacant lot behind the garage and the back of the diner. She had walked parallel to the buildings lining up beside the diner and now stepped out into the field in order to turn the corner to head up the small alley that he'd said led to the front of the café. It was at that moment she spotted the black-and-white cat. She loved cats, and they loved her.

"Hey, little kitty." She stepped forward toward the scraggly bush not too far from the porch. She bent down to get a better look at the cat, to coax it out so she could pet it. Black beady eyes blinked at her from beneath the bush…she froze and swallowed hard as her eyes caught the white stripe running from between those eyes and running the length of the black skunk. "A, a skunk."

"Straighten up slowly," a very masculine voice instructed her from somewhere to her left.

She had no options and was grateful for instructions because she had never been practically nose-to-nose with a stinky skunk before and had no clue what her options were. *Maybe if she ran, it could catch her like a bear would do. Could skunks run that fast?*

Her heart thundered as she swallowed her fear and desire to make a dash for it. Instead, she slowly straightened up and out of the corner of her eye, she saw a cowboy—*oh goodness, what a cowboy*. He stepped slowly off the porch. Her gaze darted to him and for a moment she forgot why she was standing frozen like an icicle behind the café.

He was tall, had black hair, tanned skin made even darker by the crisp white cotton shirt he wore with well-worn, starched jeans that ended at shiny buffed boots the color of rich mahogany. But that wasn't what stole her mind. It was the vibrant green eyes that bore into her with serious intent, mesmerizing her, or hypnotizing her to do as he said. Right now, she'd do just about anything he told her to do, even if there wasn't a skunk at her feet.

Skunk at my feet. Her gaze shifted at lightning speed to the beady-eyed creature glaring up at her. She flinched, knowing in that instant she was done. In a quick flick, its tail shot up and the little beast hopped around and aimed—

In that same instant, strong hands grasped her around the waist as the handsome cowboy yanked her close to his rock-hard body and swung them around so he shielded her from the stout rank scent that exploded from back of the awful black-and-white fluffball.

The scent filled the air. Maisy covered her nose while at the same time completely aware that she was being shielded by the cowboy. *What a nice guy. Amazing, really, that he'd done something so nice. Then again there was probably no way she was walking away from this smelling like a rose. Nope, a toilet maybe, but no rose.*

But him...oh dear goodness, he stunk, and he stunk bad.

"I told you not to move," he growled into her ear, his breath warm against her skin.

"I didn't," she bit back as the shock of what had just happened settled over her like the scent seeping into their pores.

Without another comment, he swung her into his arms; she gasped as he strode forward, away from the nasty scent that hovered in the air. He didn't stop until they were around the corner of the diner in the alley that she'd been headed to when she'd been distracted by the skunk.

"What in tarnation were you thinking in the first place when you went after that skunk?" he demanded in a not-so-very-nice tone.

"I thought it was a cat."

"Well, clearly you need to have your eyes checked."

They had come around the corner but they were not smelling any better considering the scent had followed them. Her eyes were burning and her nose had started to burn too.

"It was black and white. It was an easy mistake."

"If you say so. I had been waiting for that blamed skunk all morning. Your mistake cost me, in more ways than one." He set her on her feet and stuffed his hands on his hips as he glared down at her. His very nice nose crinkled in defense of the scent. "This is bad."

"Yes, it is." She stepped back from him, testing the possibility that she might not smell as horribly as he did. Feeling guilty at the same time that he had taken the brunt of the hit. Her own nose crinkled as if trying to shrink away from the smell too. She wrapped a hand around the back of her neck and rubbed the tight muscles. "What are we going to do?"

"I think we need to get this stink off of us."

"How? It's awful, will it come off?"

His lip twitched, and he almost smiled. "Lots of tomato sauce is in our futures. Although, I have to say it didn't help all that much when I was a kid and this happened."

The very thought this wasn't coming off was horrifying. The smell seemed to be intensifying. "But, I don't have a place to do that. My ride and my travel trailer are at the repair place being fixed. I was going to check into a bed-and-breakfast after I ate."

His brows dipped over his serious eyes. "Well, then, I guess we head down to Sally Ann's place. Maybe she can get you the room on the back of the bed-and-breakfast so you don't run all her other guests off."

That would be terrible. "I wouldn't want to do that." She was about to show up and possibly get turned away because she could run off the poor woman's other patrons. *What would she do? Go back to her travel trailer and take a shower while it was being repaired?* "This is not good."

His nose crinkled, making the handsome features relax slightly. "Tell me about it. But Sally Ann can help, or I can call in the cavalry. You'll be okay. I'm Drake Presley, by the way."

"I'm Maisy Love."

"That's really your last name?"

"That's really my last name."

"I guess that's not so bad for a woman but I'd hate to be a man with a moniker like that."

She laughed. "I see your point." There were a lot of other names out there that could be worse, but she didn't point that out. "Who is the cavalry?"

"My family. We'll take care of you." He started walking down the alley toward the front of the diner and she followed him. The man had a walk that was decisive, long strides and with purpose. As if he'd made a decision and now he was implementing it and nothing better get in his way. She followed him, pretty certain herself that she didn't want to get left behind, standing on the sidewalk of the main road with people looking at her and wondering why she smelled so horrible. That would be humiliating.

There were cars and trucks pulled into the slanted parking spaces that lined the street. The diner, or café since that was what was on the sign, looked busy this morning. There were a few people coming out of the place as they rounded the corner. A couple of cowboys laughed as they talked about something. The moment they saw them, they stopped talking and their gazes locked on them. Surprise registered on their handsome faces and they took a step back.

"Drake, what in the world? Did you tangle with a polecat?" The surprise turned to a grin and the cowboy's eyes twinkled with laughter as he swiped his hat from his head and fanned it toward them to ward off the scent permeating from them.

"I think it's obvious I did." He frowned. His gaze shifted to her, and she thought she saw apology in their beautiful depths. "Fella's this is Maisy Love. And Maisy, these are my brothers, Shane and Cooper, pay no attention to him." He indicated Cooper with a sharp nod.

Cooper's eyes lit with devilish mirth. "I couldn't help but tease my older brother. He's a little uptight, if you haven't noticed. And normally he knows how to avoid skunk spray so I'm curious about how or what distracted him."

"That's my fault. He was trying to keep it off of me. I'm afraid I'm the one who didn't see it coming." She grimaced and hated that she'd caused this. She caught Drakes jaw tense and his gaze narrow as it drilled into Cooper. She was more intrigued but also felt bad.

"Not a problem. He'll live," Shane said, eyeing her with concern. "That's pretty bad, though. It's going to be rough getting rid of that scent."

"Tell us about it. And I'm not sure that's going to do the job." Drake frowned. He reached a hand out and cupped her elbow. "We're heading to Sally Ann's and see if she has a place for Maisy, maybe at the back so she doesn't disturb the other guests."

"Jenna is there. They'll fix her up. You'll be in good hands."

Maisy hoped so. She was starting to feel nauseous. The scent was starting to overpower her instead of her getting used to it. And he had her worrying that they might not be able to get rid of it. "We better go before we both pass out from the smell."

"Yeah, y'all might need to get that off as quick as possible. How about me and Shane go to the store and pick up some more supplies?" Cooper asked, grimacing while his eyes crinkled at the edges.

Drake's nose twitched. "That'd be great. Get a lot. Enough for me and for Maisy. I don't have any in my cabinets. And stop grinning."

"I'm not grinning."

"Your eyes are about to tear up you're holding back so much laughter."

Cooper laughed. "Okay, so I can't help myself. But I'm on my way to your rescue. I'll run yours by your house and Shane can bring Maisy's by the B&B."

"Sounds like a plan."

She was relieved. It sounded as though she might get this gone soon. There would be no interviewing at the Goodnight Café until she didn't smell like a garbage dump.

Drake was quiet as he took Maisy to the B&B. He wondered about her but didn't ask questions. He could tell by the fact that she was starting to turn a tinge of green that she needed to have this skunk scent off her and soon. When they arrived at Sally Ann's, both women were waiting on the porch. He knew immediately that Shane had called his wife, Jenna, and told her what was coming. He wondered who was watching their store across the street.

Sally Ann's grin was as bright as a high-powered spotlight as she watched them walk up the steps to the yellow house with the colorful porch furniture. Jenna was smiling too and there was a teasing twinkle in her eyes.

"Whew, you two sure know how to make an entrance. Drake, what'd you do to this poor girl?" The junk store and B&B owner fanned the air in front of her face, her nose crinkled.

"We found Gert's skunk," Drake said, in no mood to tease.

"Did you get it?"

He frowned and his gaze shifted automatically to Maisy. "Nope. It got away."

Maisy's pale-eyes had a lavender hue, and they flashed a deeper shade as she turned rose. "That would be my fault." Exasperation rang in her tone.

"There will be another chance." Jenna glared at Drake. "I'm sure my brother-in-law won't let a little skunk get the better of him."

"I'll get it. But first, we have to get rid of the stench it gifted us with. Sally Ann and Jenna, this is Maisy Love. She walked up on the skunk while I was about to trap it."

"And it sprayed you both?" Jenna looked sympathetic while starting to fan the air in front of her nose too.

"No, he tried to protect me and took most of the hit." Maisy looked embarrassed, and he felt bad for her while something in his chest tightened. "I was on the way from the repair shop to the diner and then I was going to come here and get a room if you have one. I met the skunk instead. I thought it was a cat."

Sally Ann and Jenna both looked baffled at her words. He understood their look. Despite the irritating fact that she'd caused all of this, he felt bad for her having been sprayed. But, the fact that she was clueless about the difference in a black-and-white cat and a black-and-white skunk...well, he'd ignore that because he couldn't fathom how anyone could make that mistake. Obviously, Sally Ann and Jenna were having the same struggle.

"I'm not a country girl. I've never seen a skunk up close," she said, as if realizing what they were all thinking. "Anyway, do you have a room? Can you help me? If not, I guess I'll have to get some tomato sauce and find a creek somewhere."

"Of course, we're going to help you," both ladies said at the same time.

"But tomato sauce is just a myth. It takes baking soda, peroxide, and dishwashing detergent to get it off skin and animals. I've got enough to fix you up, but just in case, they're bringing backup."

"I'm glad you know what to do," Maisy said. "We don't have to pretend to be spaghetti." She smiled brightly at him.

Those teasing eyes tempted him.

"Good to know. Thank you, ladies. I'm heading out." Drake tipped his hat at Sally Ann, then met Maisy's gaze before he headed back the way he'd come.

He couldn't get out of there fast enough.

CHAPTER TWO

"Go back in there. You still stink, dude," Cooper grunted as soon as Drake walked out of the bathroom with a towel around his hips.

"I cannot rub down with that concoction any longer," he growled. "I've got things to do." He was not happy with one Miss Maisy Love. "Tell me, Coop, when you see a skunk, you know it's not a cat. Right?"

"Well yeah, but I'm a cowboy. You said she was a city gal. I'm guessing maybe that's why she saw the black and white fur in the bushes and thought cat. Maybe her view didn't allow her to see that the white was a stripe attached to a thick tail."

He shot his brother a glare.

"You can glare at me all you want but you need to

get back in there and dunk yourself in a tub of that stuff if you have to. And stay there till you smell better."

"How long is this supposed to take? I've got things to do—"

Cooper took him by the shoulders and turned him around. "Right now, big brother, you have only one thing to focus on and that's how you smell." Cooper laughed as he shoved Drake through the door then pulled the door shut with a firm snap. "Don't come out till you smell better."

Disgusted, but unable to take the scent any longer, Drake walked back into the bathroom and growled as he started rubbing down with the slimy goop he'd mixed up in the sink. This was as bad as slipping in a cattle trailer after a load of cattle had just unloaded. Okay, maybe this wasn't as bad as that but at least cow manure washed off with soap.

He'd be lucky if this came off at all.

"So how do you feel?" Sally Ann asked as Maisy walked out of the bathroom a couple of hours later.

"Better, if I don't smell. Do I? I don't smell it anymore but then, I might have gotten used to it." Maisy laughed at the thought of growing used to the perfume of skunk.

"Naw," the older woman said with a wave of her hand and a wide smile. "You smell great. Now sit down here and let's have a nice slice of my lemon pound cake and coffee, or tea if you prefer."

Maisy wasn't sure how she had lucked out so well on this ordeal, to have landed at this lovely lady's darling bed-and-breakfast. Sally Ann was a doll and so was Jenna, her niece. But she had. There couldn't be nicer people anywhere and they'd really come to her rescue. "Thank you, I would love a slice of that. It looks absolutely delicious."

"They tell me it is. I personally could drink the lemon glaze, but I don't since it wouldn't be too good for me in large doses."

"I can't wait to taste it. And coffee sounds fabulous."

She slid into the seat at the table of the brightly colored kitchen that looked as if it had been decorated with style from an era of long ago. There was an assortment of colored vintage items used on the countertops.

Sally Ann poured coffee into a large mug. "I think china cups are lovely, for tea. When I want coffee, I want a mug."

"I agree. Thank you. So…" She paused to take a sip of the hot liquid. "Oh, perfect. That hits the spot. So, have you lived here long?"

"Yes, I claim it home. Now, my Jenna just moved here. She's back over at the store taking care of some things for me while I take care of you. And the other guests. But most of them are over at the shop or the other stores in town. We are getting more and more day trippers out of the city lately, and making this little town a destination for antiquing, or junkin'—as I like to call it. What brings you to be passing through town?"

"I am a blogger and I do an online show on diners in small-town America. I travel to the destinations and then do interviews with the owners and we cook together. I was on my way to Fredericksburg when this happened. Now, since I'm sidelined with a broke-down transportation, I'm thinking the Goodnight Café might be an excellent detour for the show. What do you think?"

"It would be wonderful. Gert, the owner, is my good buddy and you'll have fun with her. Though she doesn't do all the cooking anymore, they are all her recipes. You won't find any bread pudding anywhere in the country better than hers. I mean, she has a bunch of great food but that is a specialty passed down through her family from years back."

Bread pudding sounded like the perfect segment for the show. If Sally Ann raved this much about it, then it was probably every bit as good as she said. "My mouth is watering for a taste already. But this lemon pound cake is as good as I thought, too. How would you feel about me having a show with cooking with you too? I mean, I'm here and your B&B is so warm and welcoming. I know my viewers would enjoy knowing they could come to Ransom Creek and stay here and do their junkin' and eating at the same time." She smiled, seeing the shows in her mind as she spoke.

She was pleased about the progress and the fact that the skunk had gotten her would be a fun segment. The thought that maybe she could get the handsome cowboy in the show somehow flashed through her thoughts. *Probably not.* He had the look of a man who wouldn't appreciate being on camera. Still, a girl could hope. There was no denying cowboys in the background of the diner would be a nice bit of scenery that the viewers weren't used to.

"I think I'd love that. And I'm always looking for ways to get the word out about the B&B. Jenna is doing my marketing for me now and that has helped, but this sounds like a gift from heaven. Gert's going to be as happy as I am about our 'luck' that you broke down here."

"Wonderful. I know I am. It's always a real adventure when I happen upon a special place and something tells me that Ransom Creek is special. And that your B&B is going to be a big hit. The diner, too, and I haven't been there yet." She took another bite of the delicious cake and almost groaned. It was so amazing and light, not to leave out how the lemony goodness made her smile as she chewed. She'd hit pay dirt when she'd landed in Ransom Creek.

"What did you think about our Drake Presley? He's a catch, don't you think?"

The sly question slipped right in there between comments as Sally Ann took a small bite of cake herself and washed it down with a sip of hot coffee while watching Maisy intently over the rim of her red mug. It was so calculated, it was funny. Maisy smiled warily. "He's a cutie, I'll admit that. But I hope you aren't getting your hopes up about any matchmaking or something resembling matchmaking because I'm not your woman for that. I've got places to be and sights to see."

Sally Ann frowned, her brows making horizontal question marks over her eyes. "You're telling me that in all this traveling you do, you are not on the lookout for Mr. Right?"

"No, I'm not looking for Mr. Right, Wrong, or Perfect. I'm tending to my own agenda and it doesn't have room in it for a personal life, right now." The sight of him stepping in to take the hit from the skunk slammed into Maisy—she quickly shoved it right back out of her mind.

That got a frown from the B&B owner as she set her cup down. "You are really eating into my fun here." She laughed and shook her head.

"I'm sorry. Maybe tomorrow someone else will show up who is perfect for your plans."

She took the delicious cake and wondered whether the handsome cowboy had a clue that he was the target of a matchmaking setup. Then again, maybe all the single men in town were targets, and he was the one being mentioned now because he'd been the one who'd helped her.

Whatever the case, it might be fun watching him get set up.

As long as it wasn't with her.

Drake was at his desk, going over the ranch finances, three hours after the skunk fiasco. He had checked his numbers twice and still hadn't come up with the same totals. Instead of having his mind where it ought to be, he had a pretty ball of energy on his mind. He wondered whether she had been able to get rid of the skunk smell. Wondered how long she'd be in town.

The force of his desire to go to town and check on her was strong. Standing, he moved to the window and distracted himself from what was on his mind. *Why couldn't he get her off his mind? She wasn't what he was looking for—not that he was looking for anyone right now.* Maybe never, not with the gnawing fear that never left him. The one that he'd tried to deny for most of his life, at least his life after losing his mother when he was so young. He'd had the gift of having complete memories of his mother before she'd died that horrific night giving birth to his baby sister. He'd had the painful memory of how excruciating not only his heartbreak had been, but that of his dad and his brothers. And he'd coped the only way he'd known how: he'd thrown himself into the role of picking pieces up and trying to ease his dad's pain by helping him with the younger boys. It had been a nightmare for the family but they had fought their way through, mourning in different ways, but eventually made it as best they could.

The fear, though, had never left him. He was afraid of marrying and taking the risk of living the nightmare all over again. He didn't know how his dad had made it. And, his dad only just in the last year started to toy with dating. Only after he'd had a heart attack had he begun to step out and enjoy the company of Karla, the nurse who'd taken care of him in the hospital. Drake was happy for his dad, and he hoped that maybe he could move forward and take the dating to the next level and actually have a relationship and maybe a future with Karla. She was a great lady and everyone really liked her. Drake just hadn't gotten to that point yet.

The fear always darkened the edges of his world when he met someone who interested him just a little. He'd tried when he was younger to overcome it, to date some. But he'd never been able to relax and let himself enjoy himself enough to let go. And thus never dated very long. His family had it wrong. They thought he was just too preoccupied with making the ranch a success. They had no idea that their older brother was a chicken.

But he was. And until the moment he'd looked into the wide eyes of Maisy Love, he'd managed. But something felt different since meeting her. It was as if she were a huge magnet that he couldn't shake. Moving away from the window, he grabbed a hat off the wall hook, a different hat from the one that he'd had to leave hanging on a fence post to air out from the skunk fiasco, and strode outside. He needed to move, to throw himself into some physical exercise and that meant joining his brothers cutting cows from the herd to take to the sale.

He crossed the ranch yard from the office to the stable. The scent of fresh hay and horse—just entering the stable always helped calm him down and stabilize his world. Riding would help also. Growing up, he'd spent every hour he could on the back of a horse, or a bull. Though he'd not ridden bulls long, having decided his place was helping make the ranch into a powerhouse by using his understanding of finance and ranch management.

His dad had encouraged him and today, the two of

them worked the office end of the ranch while his brothers worked the ranch. But that didn't stop him from getting out and working with them when he could...or needed to.

He was riding across the pasture toward the horizon when he realized he was going to have to go back to town tonight or in the morning and catch the skunk. Even if it meant getting sprayed again...or running into Maisy.

CHAPTER THREE

The diner was packed when she walked in to have an early dinner and to meet Gert. Sally Ann had had to go back to her store, Junk to Treasure, but had told Maisy to make herself at home. Maisy planned to stop by the shop after she'd talked to Gert about an interview and hopefully a cooking segment. She loved the place the moment she entered. It was bright and homey-looking, as if it came out of an era of the past. A place where people had gathered for meals with their families and friends for decades. Glass counters filled with fluffy pies that had her mouth watering just looking at them. There were tables and booths and though not full at the moment, the cowboys sitting around a late lunch looked as if they'd just come in from the range. She guessed that was how you would say they'd just come from working on the ranch. She really didn't have a clue considering she'd never been raised on a ranch or near a ranch, despite being from Texas.

They smiled and tipped their hats. One of them reminded her of Drake Presley—the vibrant green eyes, she figured. She smiled back and then slid into a booth near the counter. Her stomach growled, reminding her that she had only eaten the lemon cake at Sally Ann's earlier. And she'd forced herself not to eat more than the large piece that her hostess had first given her. She needed to eat something more than sweets. Though she did enjoy them, she tried hard not to overindulge because she tended to feel sluggish afterward. But sometimes, like now, it was really hard to deny herself the treat.

"Hi." A young waitress greeted her as she came from the kitchen area. "I'm Libby and I'll be your server today. What can I get you? You're new in town."

"Hi Libby, I am new. Just visiting. What do you suggest?"

"Great. Hoss is cooking today, and he makes amazing food. But the applewood smoked club sandwich with Gert's famous potato salad as a side is one of my favorites. He just made one for one of the cowboys over there and it made me want one."

"That sounds like a winner. I'll have that. And I may have to try a piece of that pie when I'm done. They look amazing."

Libby's smile grew. "Thank you. Those are my specialty. I started making them for the diner about two weeks ago."

"Then I'll for certain have to try a piece."

"Let me get this to Hoss and then I'll bring you something to drink. What would you like?"

"Water with lemon, please."

Moments later, Libby was back with a large glass of ice water and several slices of lemon in a dish. "Are you the person who had the encounter with the skunk and Drake this morning?"

Maisy laughed. "Yes, that'd be me. To my horror. I was trying to come have something to eat then but got a tad delayed."

"I heard it was bad. I'm engaged to his brother, Vance. Brice over there, the cowboy who resembles him, is another brother. Not as dark-haired as Drake but you can pick him out, I'm sure."

"Yes, I thought so when I saw him. There must be a lot of them, the brothers. He'd make five if my count is right. Cooper and Shane came to our rescue with neutralization supplies."

"Yes, there's five and a sister, though she lives a few hours from here. Brice stopped by Drake's and said it took Drake a while to stop stinking." She giggled. "He's so serious all the time, I can only imagine how much he did not like that happening." She glanced over her shoulder at the table where Brice was sitting. "Brice, did you meet Maisy? She had the great adventure with Drake this morning."

That drew the table of cowboys to stop eating and look her way. Brice stood and came over toward her.

He was striking as he strode across the room, and yet there had just been something that had sparked between her and Drake the moment her gaze had met his. Brice was smiling at her and his green eyes twinkled like emeralds as he held out his hand to her. When she placed hers in the big, work-callused palm, there was no tingle of awareness dancing along her skin as had been the case when she'd met Drake.

Why could she not get the cowboy off her mind?

"I suspected when you entered you might be the woman who threw my brother's day into a tailspin. Or, I guess, your day got thrown into a tailspin too."

She laughed. "That's a good way to put it. I survived but hope that never happens again. I won't be going behind the building again, that is for certain."

"Don't worry. Drake had us pick up a bunch more of the cage traps and we eased back there and set them up. Mr. Skunk will be caught and hauled off soon. We can't have Gert or anyone else getting hurt back there again."

"That's good. I'm sure everyone will be happy." She could only imagine how determined her cowboy rescuer would be if he set his mind to it. Drake seemed like the kind of man who got things done. Brice probably could be just as determined but the light in his eyes and his easy smile told her he took life a little less serious. *Actually, that was more her style, so why was it that she had this almost magnetic pull where Drake was concerned?*

Libby nodded her agreement. "I'll be glad it's gone. And Gert will be too. She'll be back tomorrow. Maybe y'all will catch it tonight. Doc has her with her foot up today and in a brace of some sort. She'll be sitting in the front booth tomorrow greeting everyone, even if she can't wait tables or do some cooking. She loves this café and everyone who comes in, and sitting is going to drive her bonkers."

"Yeah, it is," Brice agreed. "I'm just glad she didn't break a hip or something else."

"Order up," the big man in the kitchen called, looking through the opening as he set a plate in the pass-through.

"Be right back. That's yours."

"Well, I'll let you eat in peace but it was nice

meeting you. I'll tell Drake you survived very nicely."

"I hope he did. I still feel guilty for having caused him to get sprayed so badly."

Libby returned and set Maisy's food on the table. She was smiling. "I think it's funny. Of all people, for it to happen to, Drake is the most unlikely. I love him to death but he's so serious all the time."

Brice laughed hard, mischief lighting his face. "She's right, the man needs his world shaken up a little. He's entirely too serious, and this knocked him off-balance a bit. How long are you in town for?"

She felt bad for Drake, and yet she could see what they were talking about just from the short time she'd been near him. She had an itch to loosen the cowboy up. "As long as it takes to get my ride fixed."

"Great. Maybe you can come out to the ranch for dinner one night. I'll see what I can stir up. Good to meet you. I have to get back to the ranch now before my brothers accuse me of slacking off." He winked, tipped his hat at her then gave Libby a one-armed hug. He headed back to his table, where he laid a few bills beside his plate, said goodbye to the cowboys he'd been sitting with, then headed out the door.

"That man is up to something," Libby said. "Did you see the twinkle in his eyes?"

"I did. What do you think it meant?"

Libby cocked her head to the side. "Well, I don't want to alarm you, but I think he thinks you and Drake being thrown together again might be a good thing. Bye, fellas. Thanks," she called and waved as the other cowboys laid money on their table and headed out through the heavy swinging doors, leaving the two of them as the only people in the dining room. Besides the cook, they were now alone in the café.

"Why is that? I got the same impression from Sally Ann earlier." She wasn't getting fixed up with anyone but decided there really was no need to say anything and she was curious about why they would want to.

Libby slapped her hands to her hips. "He enjoys his work, I guess. I mean, don't get me wrong, he's really nice, just quieter than his other four brothers, and he thinks hard. I haven't really been around all that long but that's how I see him. Vance is his youngest brother and they're worlds apart on personality. Vance is outgoing and says that Drake has always been very protective of all of them. As long as he can remember, Drake has been almost like a dad to him. He thinks it has something to do with losing their mom when they were kids."

"That's so sad." Her mother drove her a bit mad most of the time but it would be awful imagining the world without her. Their relationship might not be the best but she knew her mother cared for her in her own way.

"Yes. Anyway, I hope you enjoy your meal."

"Thanks. And don't forget I'm having pie."

"You just give me a wave when you're ready."

She watched Libby walk away and then bit into her sandwich. It was perfect. It also sounded like Drake was perfect too.

Stop thinking about the cowboy.

She heard the warning loud and clear, and yet…as she took another bite of the sandwich, she couldn't help wondering what it would take to put a smile on those perfect lips and a twinkle in his serious, consuming eyes.

He got the skunk bright and early the next morning and he did it without getting sprayed. He had driven to town before daylight and taken up his position to watch for the skunk. Cooper and Brice had done as he'd asked and placed six more traps around the area. It was excessive for a single varmint but if that was what it took, than that was what it took. As the sky turned pink with the coming of the new day, he spotted the deceptively innocent-looking animal ambling slowly from one trap to the other, sniffing each and then moving on. They'd also placed different bait in several of them, and his hope was one of them would be irresistible to the skunk.

As it ambled to one of the newly placed traps, it moved a bit faster, as if it caught the scent of something it liked. Drake's pulse increased with optimism and he sure hoped there was no interruption because he had a good feeling about this.

Thankfully, all remained quiet as the skunk

walked right inside the cage and straight to the peanut butter and jelly open-faced sandwich and started eating—completely unaware that he couldn't retreat back through the opening without the latch being tripped by Drake.

"Yes! About time." Grabbing the thick blanket, he opened it and held it in front of him as he walked slowly over and very carefully placed it over the cage. Once that was done, he got the piece of foot-wide plywood that he'd had waiting against the wall for this moment and took his time sliding it beneath the blanket-covered cage. He was home free now.

All he had to do now was deposit the animal somewhere in the middle of the ranch, where it could be happy and everyone else could be too.

He picked up the three-foot-long by one-foot-wide board and carried the cage to his truck. He'd parked in front of the café, not wanting to disturb the animal if it happened to be around. Now, he deposited it in the back of his truck then headed to the driver's side. Before he opened his door, he spotted a jogger running down the deserted street toward him. He knew before she got close enough to see her face that it was Maisy Love. His pulse kicked up instantly.

She wore a pair of leggings that stopped just below her knees and a bright neon-green tank that clung to her curves. Her hair was slapped on top of her head in a messy bun that left sprigs springing out about her face and he found her a refreshing mix of cuteness and beauty.

"Well howdy there, cowboy." She came to a halt near him. "Whatcha got under that blanket? Our skunk?" Her eyes were alive with teasing, making his pulse go wilder than a bucking bronc being attacked by bees.

Not that he felt as if he were being attacked by bees. Quite the contrary; he felt as though he were falling into a pool of clear cool water, looking into those crystal-clear hues of lavender.

"Got him. Now I'm taking him out to let him go."

"Are you really—can I come?"

"Do what?"

"Can I come with you? I've never seen anything like this. I'd love to experience it. If I'm not going to get sprayed again."

He wanted to tell her no but there wasn't any plausible reason to deny her. And to tell the truth, he liked the idea. "Fine with me. But don't get too close."

She clapped her hands. "This is exciting and don't worry, I'll stay inside the truck. How's that?"

"That'll work. Hop in." He watched a dazzling smile of excitement bloom across her face.

He was in trouble.

CHAPTER FOUR

What had she been thinking when she'd asked to ride along with Drake?

That you wanted to take a ride with him. True, but she should have turned around and jogged the other way when she'd spotted him. But that hadn't been an option because she'd been drawn to him. She'd wanted to go with him. To see how many times she could cause the corners of his lips to lift into a smile.

"So, where are we going?" She grinned widely at him, anticipation dancing through her like a fairy splashing in raindrops.

"Somewhere way out in the middle of the ranch. I don't want to drop him near town or in someone else's territory, so I'll drop him there and he'll have plenty of room to root around."

He cranked the engine, and they headed out toward the rising sun as it lifted from the horizon in a beautiful display of fading pink to blue. The day held promise.

She studied him, fascinated by the man. "You're a very serious cowboy." She leaned against the door, shifting her seat belt to allow her the room to do that. She wanted to see him. To watch every nuisance of his expression. Why, she couldn't really say other than it was a little like watching the still waters of a pond and waiting on the ripple after sending a rock splashing into the calmness.

He slid her a glance. "Is that a bad thing?"

She smiled mischievously. "Oh no, I don't guess. Do you make babies cry when you come into the room or when you tickle their tummies and frown?"

"What kind of question is that?" He shot her a startled glance that was almost a glare.

She laughed, her shock tactic getting a reaction that tickled her for some strange reason. She crossed her arms and cocked her head. "Well, do you?"

His frown deepened. "I don't tickle baby tummies."

The man was cute. She chuckled again. "Is that because they're crying too hard when you glare at them?"

"No, I don't glare at babies. I'm not even around babies that much. Why are you asking me this?"

Oh, he was fun to tease. "Just testing to see if I can rile you up. And I was curious about if that serious expression is your normal look. You seem very intense."

His brows dipped. "Maybe I am. There is nothing wrong with that."

"Oh, nothing at all. I agree. Although I gotta tell you that I have a real hankering to see you smile," she admitted and knew it was true. She would pay top dollar to see the man smile like he meant it.

His eyes narrowed, digging into her. "Are you normally this pushy?"

"Ha, I'm not pushy. I'm curious. And you're not a half bad-looking cowboy. If you smiled more, you'd almost be handsome," she teased. The man was drop-dead gorgeous, even with the serious expression.

To her surprise, he chuckled and his lips slipped upward just a hair. "I bet you were a little terror when you were a kid."

"I cannot tell a lie. Drove my nervous mom batty." It was slightly true. "Drove her mad, actually."

"I sympathize with her."

"See, you are funny," Maisy pointed out at his dry joke. "You're very witty."

"Thanks. It's taken me a lifetime to perfect."

"I can tell. I'm impressed." She winked when he glanced at her and then they rode in silence for a few miles.

"I guess you're settled in at Sally Ann's?"

"I am." She was pleased that he'd initiated the conversation and she hadn't had to do it. "I'm staying for a few days. I'm hoping to meet Gert today."

"I hope so. I'm worried she was hurt worse than she let on and may need to stay home longer. But it'll be hard to keep her down."

"She sounds like my kind of woman. I like tough. I try to be tough myself."

"And here I thought you were the soft and cuddly type."

"Another funny. Man, you're on a roll."

He laughed dryly. "I'm a regular stand-up comic."

"Oh, I wouldn't go that far. Though these days, from what I've seen, it wouldn't take much to be funnier than the fellas and gals on television."

"I agree with that." He slowed and turned onto a dirt road then drove over the cattle guard. "We're on Presley land."

"It's beautiful. I love seeing the scattered oak trees everywhere."

"I thought you weren't a country girl. You just named what those trees were."

"People do have oak trees in the city."

"Maybe, but I see more concrete than I'd like. I'll take wide-open spaces any day."

She'd pegged him as that from the moment she'd seen him. "If it's all this pretty, then I can totally relate. I might not ever want to leave the area after today." The statement threw her off. "I mean, I will leave. I always leave. What I meant was—"

"That you don't plan to stick around very long after your ride gets fixed."

"Exactly. You're good." She liked hearing the tiny bit of tease in his voice. She had to listen hard to find it but it was there. "Really, are you always so serious?"

He looked surprised. "No."

"I find you fascinating. Intriguing, really. I can't seem to stop looking at you and wondering when the sun is going to come out and a big smile cross that stoic face of yours."

He cocked his head to the side to look at her. "I'm not sure what to say to that."

She had the overwhelming temptation to run her fingers along his jaw. Okay, so she really wondered if she kissed him, would he loosen up? She had a feeling he would. Then again, he might shoo her right out of his truck and leave her on the side of the road with the skunk.

Instead, she smiled. "Don't say anything—just

give me a little tip of the ole lips upward. Just a little. See, you want to." It was true; his lips were tilting, slowly, slowly and bingo! He chuckled and shook his head as a smile—one of complete disbelief and bewilderment, she was certain—overtook his handsome features. Why she thought she heard alarms blaring at the same time. Alarms of caution—danger ahead.

Because it was just as she'd suspected: a smiling Drake Presley was a breathtaking, heart-stealing, dangerous man. Especially to a gal with her heart set on not getting involved.

"Oh." Maisy gasped, her eyes widening as she stared at him, causing his heart to suddenly go on a rampage inside his chest. "Why would you keep that so well hidden?"

The woman threw him off his saddle in more ways than one and he was riding sideways right now as he looked at her. *She was trouble, all right. Already said she was leaving.* So this sudden impulse was not good, this need to pull her into his arms and kiss her in order to prove he wasn't the stone-cold cowboy she thought him to be. *Nope, not good.*

"I don't. I just tend to think hard most of the time. And you're a very pushy lady." He brought the slow-moving truck to a halt. This was as good a place as any to put the skunk out. Then he could turn the truck around and take her back to town. She was way too cute, leaning against the door of his truck, smiling and teasing him. He was serious, always had been, but that didn't make him dead. "We'll set our little friend free here."

"Oh, he's no friend of mine. And I'm not pushy. We just bonded over this skunk thing and I feel an obligation to befriend you. To loosen you up because you, my friend, are wound way too tight if you forget to smile because you're thinking too hard."

That startled a laugh out of him. "I'm fine. Really."

He got out of the truck and she started to open her

53

door.

"Hey, not so fast. You said you'd wait in the truck. Remember?"

"Oh, yeah, thanks. I will do that. But hurry back and please don't bring back any scent with you. But in case you do get sprayed, you can get in the back and I'll drive you home."

"Perfect. I knew I brought you along for some reason." He was still shaking his head as he walked to the back of the truck and let the tailgate down. Then he slid the blanket-covered cage toward himself and picked it up. He carried it several feet away from the truck and set it on the ground.

"Be careful," Maisy called.

He looked over his shoulder to see her leaning out of the truck window. The breeze was playing havoc with the knot of hair on top of her head and it waved in the wind invitingly.

Distracted, he tripped on a rock and went down. The blanket flew off; the skunk whined as the cage hit the ground. His tail came up, and he got Drake with both guns as he landed on the ground beside the angry animal.

"I'm really sorry," Maisy said again as she pulled into the driveway of the house Drake was directing her to from the truck's bed. If she'd thought he looked serious before, she was wrong. The man wore a scowl that would rank with an F5 tornado. He had barely spoken to her after she'd drawn his attention and he'd tripped on the rock. If she'd just kept her mouth shut, then he wouldn't be facing his second day scrubbing skunk smell from his skin.

She really felt bad. Then again, he wasn't believing that considering her first reaction had been to laugh. She'd smacked a hand over her mouth immediately but he'd heard her and he probably would never forgive her.

"Just pull around back and let me out."

She did as he said then watched him climb from the truck bed and stride toward his back door. She scrambled out of the truck. "Can I help you?"

"No." He halted and spun toward her with a scowl. That only made him more handsome. She was losing her mind. "You've done enough. Call someone to come get you and go home. Please."

"Hardly. I cannot abandon you after causing this to happen. Do you have plenty of the miracle concoction?"

"Plenty," he growled.

"Good. Then you go in and get to soaking and I'll whip up something to eat. It'll be lunch time by the time you get out of there."

"I'm not hungry."

"Oh stop. I've already said I was sorry. Over and over again. Now the least I can do is feed you to make up for my goof. And that's it. End of story. I'm stranded here and not leaving. You, my friend, are stuck with me."

His eyes narrowed. "Perfect. My lucky day just got better." With that, he stalked onto the porch and went inside, slamming the door behind him.

"Well, that did not go so well." She waited a few seconds, giving him time to get into the bathroom and hopefully the scent with him, and then she opened the door and went inside.

Hopefully, he had something in his pantry that she could prepare a decent meal. It was the only way she could show him how sorry she was and maybe make amends to him. Poor guy had gotten sprayed twice, the second time as bad as the first. She just hoped the scent came off this time too.

Until the moment she'd distracted him and disaster had happened, she'd been thoroughly enjoying teasing him. *Serious dude was seriously cute when perplexed.* And she was quite certain she perplexed him.

Her phone rang as she was pulling hamburger meat from the freezer. She set the package of meat on the counter then tugged her phone from her jeans pocket. It was her mom. For a brief instant, she was tempted not to answer, but that wasn't an option. "Mom, hi."

"So where are you now?"

The accusation that she was never where she was supposed to be was apparent in her mother's words.

The insinuation was always there. "I'm in a lovely little town called Ransom Creek. You'd love it. Lots of handsome cowboys and some great stores to explore for treasures."

"You say that about all the little places you visit. Aren't you supposed to be somewhere else? That's not the name I remember."

The idea that her mother would remember the name of any place she was supposed to be was almost laughable. But she was right that this wasn't her original destination, so Maisy would give her points for that. "You're right. I was heading for Fredericksburg but had a little trouble with my rig."

"You mean that dump that you call a trailer. When are you going to settle down, find a man and give me some grandchildren? I'm not getting any younger, you know."

"Mom, first it was my Jeep that had the problem. And last year you were saying you were too young to be a grandmother. And my answer is the same today as it was last week. I may never marry. But if I do, I have no idea when. Later is all I know. I have to meet the right man first." Drake's penetrating gaze filled her thoughts and sent a tingle of attraction through her. She denied it immediately.

"You just have to be open to a relationship in order for it to happen. When I met your father, there was no doubt that we were meant for each other. But I had been ready to settle down all of my life. I was ready. He was ready. That alone helps chemistry along."

Was that why, since her father's death, her mother had one Mr. Right after another? She was tempted to point out that he must not have been all that if her mother seemed to have a lot of chemistry with a lot of Mr. Rights. The old ache knotted in her stomach. If her mother had loved her dad so much, then why was she constantly with a man on her arm and the first one being only six months after her father died? No, Maisy couldn't see it as her mother did. And there was a rift growing wider and wider between them.

"Is there something you needed to talk to me about or did you just call to point out that my life isn't what you'd like it to be?"

The words were harsh. She regretted them immediately but couldn't pull them back. She was old enough to make her own decisions; her mother was making her own despite how wrong Maisy felt they were.

"I just called to check up on you. To…to hear your voice." There was a hollowness to her mother's voice that hadn't been there before.

"Is everything okay?" She wished things were right between them. Wished the clock could turn back and she could have her father back and her mother the way it used to be.

"Everything is fine…Maisy, I don't mean to push. I just wish—"

"It's fine, Mother. Maybe we'll get together after I get these next few blogs done."

"Yes, that would be good. I'd like you to meet Hank. He's nice."

She had no desire to meet Hank. The man her mother had been with for longer than any of the others—that at least was saying something, but still, she just couldn't deal with it.

They said their good-byes and then she went back to getting lunch prepared. Moments later, Drake entered the room, dressed and smelling like a tangy mix of manly cologne with a faint hint of chemical. And looking better than a cowboy should to a woman who was not interested.

"Something smells really good." He leaned past her to look into the pan.

He smelled even better up close. Startled at his nearness, she turned toward him. She was so taken by surprise her knees felt weak.

"How about me? Do I pass the test now?"

Oh man, did he ever. "Um, yes. You smell…good," she managed, feeling suddenly hot. Glad she hadn't said something like fabulous or delicious or something else equally embarrassing.

"Good." He smiled, and the room shrank to teensy-tiny—claustrophobic, almost—as she couldn't catch her breath suddenly.

"You smiled," she croaked.

He lowered his chin, bringing his face closer to hers as she was looking up at him. "I thought I'd prove to you that I'm not all ogre. You are fixing me a meal."

She laughed, nervous suddenly. "It was the least that I could do after getting you sprayed by a skunk twice in two days."

His deepening gaze seemed to drink her in and time seemed to stop. When his gaze dropped to her lips, she swallowed hard and tried to focus. Instead, her gaze moved to his lips, and she suddenly had visions of flinging her arms around his neck and yanking him close and kissing him.

Alarm bells clanged in her head and she stepped back. *What was wrong with her?*

This was so out of character for her. She was used to being in control. No man had ever caused her to lose control. She teased when she wanted to and remained completely coherent around all men. She was feeling very much less than coherent now.

He stepped back too as if he heard the same bells she was hearing. And thank goodness for that.

"After all that scrubbing, I'm starved."

"Great," she said, hastily. She picked up one of the plates she'd set on the counter beside the stove and held it out to him like a barrier between them. "Load up and have a seat. I hope you don't mind that I made myself at home in your kitchen and rummaged through your cabinets and pantry. Which, I may say, are about as neat as I had suspected they would be."

He took the plate. Their fingers touched as she passed it to him. Tingles, drat the things, danced through her, continuing to let her know that there was a female part of herself that until this moment she'd pretty much believed was immune in some way from men.

"Am I making you nervous?"

"N-no." She scoffed. "Why would you think that?" His brow hitched and those eyes darkened and the dancing tingles went wild. "Okay, maybe a little."

"Payback is tough, isn't it? You tried earlier to throw me off-balance. I have to admit knowing I can do the same to you is powerful stuff."

"So, that's what you're doing? You were purposefully yanking my chain?"

He laughed, scooped a mass of spaghetti into his plate, and then winked at her.

She had been had.

CHAPTER FIVE

He had lost his ever-lovin'-mind from all the peroxide fumes or maybe the combination of mixing baking soda, peroxide, and detergent. That had to be it because the moment he'd entered the kitchen and smelled that heavenly scent of Italian sauce and herbs and saw her standing at his stove, something had come over him that had just taken over. He couldn't have stopped his forward movement to crowd her space and lean in close if he'd wanted to. And once he'd been close enough to see the deep navy specks sprinkled sparingly in the depths of her lavender eyes, all he could think about was kissing her.

And he'd shaken her up. He'd knocked her off-balance in her saddle and it had suddenly felt good knowing that he could bewilder her like she bewildered him.

And now, sitting at the table near her as they ate, he still had kissing on his mind. One of them was going to have to come to their senses soon or this afternoon was going to go out of control. And that couldn't happen.

He stuffed another forkful of the best-seasoned spaghetti he'd ever eaten into his mouth and chewed as he willed himself to think of anything but kissing her pink lips. "I see why you cook with everyone. You're a great cook. Did your mom teach you to cook like this?"

"It's just spaghetti. But, to answer your question, no, my mom has a lot of talent with paints and colors but not food. I learned from my dad. He was an amazing cook. He had a knack with herbs. I used to stand in a chair beside him as he sprinkled a little of this and a little of that over a dish and then would let me taste the difference."

"You must have gotten his knack. You said used to. Did he die?" A sad smile told him he was right. "I'm sorry for your loss. Were you young?"

"No, it happened three years ago. It was sudden and unexpected. A drunk driver ran him off a bridge and they both ended up in the river. He dove back in to get the drunk out of his truck. The drunk came up but Daddy didn't."

Drake lost his appetite and set his fork down. Taking in the pain in her eyes. "I'm sorry."

She toyed with her meal looking as if she were trying to compose herself. At last she gave a sad smile that cut to his core. "Me too. I haven't fully recovered and I'm the first to admit it."

Compelled by a kindred spirit, he reached across the table and covered her hand with his. "You have to mourn at your own pace. Recover at your own pace. That was a terrible blow."

Her gaze lifted from where she'd been studying his hand on hers. Tears brightened her eyes. "Sorry, I don't talk about this, ever. I don't know why I messed up a perfectly good meal by opening up about it."

He gently squeezed her hand. "I'm glad you did. I lost my mother when I was a kid. I'm not over it either. I cope with it but I miss her every day. And I'll always have regrets about her not being here. My little sister has always had some guilt over Mom dying giving birth to her and that was really hard. But all in all, we've each made it through her loss in our own way. You have to do the same thing where your dad is concerned." He rubbed his thumb across her hand, hoping to impart some comfort.

"Thank you. I'm sorry for your loss. I'd heard that your mother had died. That's sad. I'm sure it was hard on all of you."

He realized he was starting to like the feel of her skin more than just comforting her and pulled his hand away. "Do you have siblings?"

"No, just me and my mom."

"How is she doing?"

She frowned, and he was startled by her eyes hardening. "Fine," she said flippantly. "She moved on quickly. Got over it within six months. I had thrown myself into my cross-country cooking idea about a month after Dad died. Working was a lifesaver for me. But about six months after we buried him, she called and said she'd met a man, the most wonderful man in the world. And that was that. Since then, she's met about five most-wonderful-men-in-the-world."

Bitterness edged her words with brittle clarity. "I'm sorry."

She took a bite of noodles and sauce. "It's fine," she mumbled. She took another bite and studied her meal.

He figured that was a signal she didn't want to talk about it. The strain between her and her mother was obvious.

His dad, on the other hand, hadn't dated. Not much anyway and had said he wasn't ready. His dad was a good-looking cowboy as a young man and still was. There had been plenty of women who'd tried to get his attention but he'd been devoted to his kids and the ranch. And his own mourning, Drake suspected. He'd only just started dating about a year ago, after the heart attack. Drake had been glad something good had come from the ordeal. He wished only good things for his dad.

"Well, your dad must have been a good man, a brave man to do what he did."

She paused and nodded. "He was. Thanks. So, back to a lighter subject. I'm thinking it's time for me to go back to town. I'm sure you're ready to get back to whatever it is you ranchers do during the day. And Sally Ann is probably wondering where I disappeared to."

She stood and moved to the trash to scoot the small bit of food on her plate into the bin. He took his over and did the same.

"I'll clean up after I take you to town. It'll be fine till then. That'll give the food time to cool off. Then I'll put it in the icebox so I can eat the rest for supper."

She smiled at that. "Okay, that sounds good. The more you enjoy it, the less terrible I can feel about putting you through such a stinky ordeal twice."

"Come on, and stop worrying. I'm over it. Just make me a deal that if I'm anywhere near and you see a skunk that you'll run and leave me out of it."

"That's a deal. Believe me, I don't want a repeat either."

He held the door for her and he had to deny the desire to give her a hug as she passed by him. She was leaving, and he had no plans for a relationship.

Therefore, hugging was not in the plan.

"This is going to be fun. I can't believe you really want to feature the café!" Gert Goodnight blinked incredulously at Maisy from across the table of the front booth. She wore a boot to protect her swollen ankle, and she had it propped up on a chair.

"Yes, it's going to be fun. I'm so glad you're going to do the show. My viewers are going to love you. What do you want to cook or bake? I've heard your bread pudding was to die for."

"It's my specialty, only because everyone loves it. But we do pies now too. And Hoss is a great cook. His cakes are amazing. I don't even attempt a cake anymore because his are so good."

"I've already asked Libby if she'd do a pie show

with me. And Hoss can cook, I have found that out already. Do you think he'd do a segment with me?"

"Nope," he called from the back. Obviously, her voice had carried. "I cook back here, not on TV or the internet. But thank you anyway."

She grinned at the big man. "You would probably be an internet sensation."

"Right. I'll keep that in mind." He grinned, tugged his hat low and went back to work.

"I should have known," Gert said. "He likes working behind the scenes."

"That's just the way it is for a lot of people."

The door opened and Sally Ann and another lady entered.

"Hey girls, come on over." Gert grinned big. "Trudy, have you met Maisy?"

The plump, pleasant-faced woman looked excited as she gave Maisy a once-over. "I came to town to find the woman who has managed to befuddle my Drake. He's untouchable and suddenly he's distracted and forgetful. This morning he came for breakfast at the big house—he has his own home, you know—but he came and I asked him several questions that he didn't hear me ask. It was so cute to see. Cooper filled me in on the great skunk caper. I think it's fabulous. And it's all because of you, so I rushed here as soon as I could get away."

Drake distracted. For some reason, this pleased her. Maisy wanted to smile, but she fought it down because she didn't want to alert the ladies that the idea thrilled her. Besides, she was still confused about how she reacted to Drake. She'd opened up about her mom and dad to the man, for goodness' sake. She never did that with anyone. It was too deep and hurt too much. And she'd just rattled off her deepest, darkest heart moments to him.

And he'd listened with empathy and he'd reached out to her with a gentle, comforting hand. And he'd touched her heart in doing so.

"Maisy, earth to Maisy."

She pulled her thoughts away from Drake and looked at Sally Ann, who was grinning broadly. "I'm sorry, what?"

"I asked if you had seen him since yesterday when

you and him ran off to set the skunk free?"

"Oh, no, ma'am. I haven't seen him. I spent yesterday afternoon working on my blog, editing some of the other interviews I've done, getting them ready to release." She'd done that but she'd also had some much-needed time alone because she'd been thrown off by the emotions that his touch and his empathy had evoked in her.

Sally Ann and Trudy looked at each other and then at Gert. She suspected that there was some matchmaking going on and she thought it was sweet. The big, serious cowboy had people who loved him and wanted to see him happy. That touched her and pleased her. Of course, it wouldn't be her because she wasn't staying. Despite the fact that he'd caused her to feel more with the gentle touch of his hand than she'd felt in years, she was still leaving.

She had to.

The ladies pulled up chairs. Libby came from the back and took their orders. The front door opened and a herd of cowboys entered. They were straight in from work, still wearing chaps and spurs. She'd seen them dusting themselves off outside when she'd glanced toward the window moments before they entered. She wondered whether Drake was working cattle today or in his office. She wondered whether he was still distracted.

She wondered when she would see him again. The questions hovered.

Libby had brought Trudy and Sally Ann tall glasses of iced tea.

"Vance is coming home tomorrow." Trudy patted her arm as she set the tea on the table. "But I'm sure you already know that."

Libby blushed. "I do. He told me when we were talking last night. I'm so excited I can hardly stand it."

"I'm sure he feels the same way. I have to say that I'm thrilled the two of you found each other because we get to see a lot more of him in between rodeos. And he's happier and so are you, and that's what matters the most."

"They're going to have that wedding soon," Gert added.

"Yes, we're deciding when the best time is."

"Good, glad to hear it," Sally Ann added.

Libby was still blushing as she walked away to take care of the table of cowboys. Maisy liked the quiet woman and was glad she'd found Vance too. From what she'd heard from Sally Ann, she'd had a hard background before arriving in town and things had been rocky with her getting settled here. But Vance had swept her off her feet, basically.

They were going to do a pie segment tomorrow, and she thought it would be loads of fun. If she could get Libby used to the camera and not feeling self-conscious.

Just as she was taking a sip of her iced tea, the door opened and Sally Ann nudged her in the ribs. She looked up and met the penetrating gaze of Drake. Excitement raced through her as everything faded around her and she felt as though it were just the two of them in the room. Heat swept through her and she sighed.

"That is one tall drink of water right there," Gert muttered from across the table and winked at Maisy.

Trudy giggled. "He's my nephew, but that is an

undeniable fact. And as stable as they come. Some lucky woman is going to win his stubborn heart one day and be very blessed indeed."

The object of their comments strode their way and swept his hat from his head to hold it against his chest. "Ladies," he said, nodding respectfully. His fingers tapped the brim of his hat and she found herself staring at those fingers, remembering the tingle they caused each time they brushed against her skin anytime they touched. *She had to stop thinking about that*, she admonished herself, and then made the mistake of meeting his gaze. Heat rushed to her cheeks.

The way they were being watched, she knew everyone witnessed the blush of her skin and the warmth in his gaze. *Perfect. These matchmakers would get ideas about them.*

Ideas that could go nowhere.

"Thank you for catching that varmint for me." Gert smiled up at him. "You're my hero, especially since you took two different shots from the sour-smelling critter." She leaned forward and breathed deeply. "I have to tell you, though, you smell good.

What in the world is that cologne you have on? I think I want some of that to just take a whiff of now and again."

"It's just something I picked up."

Maisy fought a smile, seeing how uncomfortable Gert was making him. It was cute. Which was a weird thing to say about Drake Presley. The man was tall, broad, and all male. Cute was not a descriptor she would have used until now. Unable to help herself, she leaned toward him and sniffed. "I have to agree with Gert. You smell good. Better than the last two times I was near you. I much prefer this."

"I'm glad you ladies approve. I prefer it, too. I have to admit I put the cologne on because I still smell the skunk scent."

Sally Ann looked at him with sympathy. "Poor fella. It's just because you breathed the stuff so much. It'll get better. Maybe you need to stick your nose in a can of coffee. The scent will reset your sense of smell."

"That's right," Trudy exclaimed. "It works when you are testing out different perfumes."

Drake looked slightly amused by the ladies and Maisy enjoyed seeing him relax. She just enjoyed seeing him. His gaze rested on her and her mouth went dry as flour.

"I guess you're setting up your shows?"

"I am. Libby is tomorrow and then if Gert feels able to stand a little, we're going to do hers before the weekend. We could do your show before I go, too, you know." She smiled up at him, unable not to tease him.

"I'm not cooking."

"What is it with the men not wanting to cook?" Trudy huffed.

"Drake, you know, you could do something with barbeque. All my nephews can grill to perfection but Drake has a real knack with barbeque."

"Thanks, Aunt Trudy, but I'm not cooking publicly."

"I agree," Hoss called from the kitchen. "Stick to your guns, Drake. They tried to rope me into that too."

Maisy had a sudden idea. "I've just been inspired. I usually cook with café and diner owners but I bet my viewers would enjoy me interviewing some authentic cowboys with real cowboy food. Like you barbequing. Maybe I could talk you and your brothers into each grilling a specialty."

His brows dipped as all the ladies began exclaiming excitedly that it was a great idea.

"I believe that is my cue to leave. Beth wanted us to pose for a calendar holding her goats and that's got about the same chance of happening as any of us cooking on a video."

"The goats she dresses up? That would be so awesome. You would be a hit." She smiled at him. His expression turned stormy as his eyes drilled through her and Trudy, Gert, and Sally Ann started talking at once with excited declarations about what fun it would be.

"You are not helping," he growled.

"It would loosen you up. I think we could do barbeque, with the goats roaming around in their little outfits. Big cowboy, sweet goats. My viewers would love it. Might even get me some big exposure just from all the views I would get."

"No. Can I talk to you outside?" He reached down

and cupped her elbow.

Tingles erupted through her and she stood up just from reaction. He didn't step back so their bodies were a breath apart as she looked up at him. "Why do you need me outside?"

"I need to talk to you."

"Sure." She would probably go anywhere with him at the moment. Her heart raced at his nearness, despite that he looked aggravated.

"Why don't you ask her to dinner while you're out there?" Gert suggested then chuckled.

"That's a great idea," Trudy sang.

"A tremendous idea," Sally Ann agreed with enthusiasm. "You two make a striking couple. You would make beautiful babies together."

Maisy gasped. "Sally Ann."

"I'm just stating the facts. With your dark hair and beauty, and Drake's dark good looks, babies would be striking. Toss those heather eyes of yours and his emerald, and no telling what gorgeous color eyes they'd have."

Drake tugged on her arm and headed toward the

door without saying anything. She almost ran to keep up with him because now she wanted out of there as much as he did. *What had she started?*

Once they were outside, he kept walking until they were in the alley beside the diner. Then he spun and backed her up against the building.

"What were you thinking?" he snapped.

"I was just teasing. I had no idea they'd jump on it like rabid dogs. Wow. They are some serious matchmakers."

"Tell me about it. They've been getting worse ever since my brothers started getting married. It's like they got the fever or something. And you encouraged them."

"I have to agree. Their eyes practically glazed over with excitement."

He leaned close. The scent of the cologne wafted over her. Her gaze riveted to his lips and that deep longing to feel them on hers swept through her. Butterflies erupted in her stomach and rose upward to fill her chest. She inhaled sharply, and filled her lungs completely with his scent.

"I'm not ever marrying."

His shocking declaration and his nearness caused her breaths to come quickly. "W-why?" she managed and her hand went to cover his heart. "Why would you say that?"

They stood there in that silent alley alone, so close. His emerald eyes drilled into hers, with an intensity that caused an ache to fill her.

"Because it's true. So, whether you stick around or you leave tomorrow, their matchmaking hopes are null. Void. Not happening."

Void. The word etched across her heart. "You would be a wonderful father. Why would you want to leave a void in your life like that?" she asked, using his word choice.

He placed a hand on the wall beside her head and leaned nearer, cocooning her in a world surrounded by him. "Why would you? You know, that's what you were saying in my kitchen. What's the difference in me not wanting to settle down and you not wanting to? Some people just aren't made to marry."

"But..." Her heart clenched. Heat radiated

between them and she lifted her chin in defiance. It brought their lips close. They stood there, nose to nose, lips to lips—a breath separating them. She could feel his heart raging beneath her hand and it caused hers to race in competing rhythm. "Why?" she asked again, not really her business but she could not help asking. She needed to know.

"Because some things in life hurt too much," he said, his voice grave with an emotion that tore at her. Their eyes clashed, and she lost her breath.

She lifted her hand from his heart to cup his jaw as she peered hard into his eyes. "I agree," she whispered. They just held each other's gaze, felt the heat of each other's breath on their skin as time ticked by. And then Drake Presley leaned closer and covered her lips with his.

His lips were warm and stole her breath. He was really kissing her. And not just a peck they took hers in a slow, firm kiss that was just as wonderful as she'd imagined his kiss would be. Her knees weakened and, unable to stop herself, she twined her arms around his neck and held on.

CHAPTER SIX

Drake was a man who had always been in control of every aspect of his life since he was old enough to and somehow, he'd just lost control and he was kissing Maisy. His thoughts muddled with the feel of her lips against his. Her fingers threaded through his hair and around his neck, clinging tightly as if holding him in place, desperate with wanting this as much as he knew he did.

Clarity suddenly seeped in and he froze. "Maisy," he muttered against her seeking lips. "This isn't going to happen and we both know it."

"Right," she mumbled, against his lips. Neither of them moved.

"Right." He drew from her lips another desperate kiss before he pulled away and forced himself to step away from her. "Don't stir them up anymore," he warned, trying to regain some semblance of sanity again. She was breathing hard and seemed to have the same struggle.

"No problem." Then she strode past him and headed out of the alley and away from the café.

"Where are you going?" he asked, trailing her, surprised she wasn't going back inside.

"To my room. Go away, Drake."

"But they're waiting for you inside." If she didn't go back inside, there was no telling what the ladies would concoct about what was going on.

"You go back in. I'm going to my room. You control your world, Drake—not mine. I'm not going back inside the diner after that kiss and think they're not going to take one look at me and know what we just did. I'm not a good poker player."

"Are you okay?"

"I'm fine. Go back to your ranch. See you later."

Something didn't feel right. She was mad. He wasn't a rocket scientist but then it didn't take one to feel the anger radiating off her.

"I'm sorry I kissed you. I didn't plan on it. It won't happen again."

She spun on him, her eyes flashing. "No, it won't, because you're right. I'm leaving and this would not work for either of us." She strode back to him and poked a finger into his chest. "Don't kiss me again, cowboy."

She was very cute mad. "I won't. And you stop teasing." He wrapped a hand around her poking finger. Her eyes widened, and he suddenly was enjoying teasing her.

She tried to yank her finger from his hand. He held on and grinned. "Poking a bear isn't safe, you know."

She swallowed and looked less confident. When she yanked again, he let go. "No teasing."

"I'll try." Her hand shot to her hip; she threw her shoulders back and challenged him. "But I have to level with you—I enjoy it too much. You are one serious cowboy and I just get an itch to loosen you up."

He was getting an itch to loosen her up. *Focus, Drake.* "Try to resist."

Their gazes locked and attraction radiated between them.

He couldn't stop staring at her. She was tempting, so tempting. But what good would it do? She was leaving, and that didn't erase the fact that he had made a pact with himself he was not going to marry. He was not taking any chances of ever having to live through what he had lived through with his family after their mother had died. *Not happening.*

"We have an agreement then. If you don't tease, I won't kiss you. So, if you don't want that, I suggest you keep that cute mouth of yours closed."

Maisy collapsed against the wall as she watched Drake walk away with long, determined strides. Her heart was so erratic, she needed a place to sit down. The man had completely undone her. *That kiss… Oh, what a kiss. And she kissed him back. How could she?* And she had egged him on. But he had been so cute when she was teasing him. And then there was the thrill of it. Seeing that spark in his serious eyes. That spark of fire and warmth.

She was a little confused.

Very confused.

Emotions, feelings she had never experienced before washed over her in waves—heat waves. Of course, it was explainable—just look at the man. *Who wouldn't find him obnoxiously attractive?* And he was turning her world into a spiral. One that she really wasn't wanting to be on. She wanted to get out of this town. She needed to get her interviews done and to get out. She had places to see, things to do. She was not messing up her life by letting a man control her emotions.

No sir, not happening.

She pulled away from the wall and placed a hand on her stomach, attempting weakly to steady the turbulence she was feeling. When she reached the sidewalk, she headed toward the B&B—no way could she go back inside the diner. They would all take one look at her and know exactly what she and Drake had done. It was embarrassing. And now that she'd seen their hearts, she knew there would probably be cheering and clapping involved. Maybe not physically but mentally there certainly would be. She could even hear it.

Matchmakers were a dangerous lot.

Relief swept over her when the bright-yellow bed-and-breakfast came into view. She hurried to the back door and up the stairs to her room. She closed the door and slumped against it, breathing easier.

Now what?

Get ready for the live video. *Yes*, there was plenty to do.

And that did not include thinking about Drake Presley. *Nope, it did not.*

But as she started to work, he was still there, boldly yanking her chain.

Drat, the cowboy.

The morning after he'd kissed Maisy, Drake was still kicking himself in the rear for losing control. He hadn't meant to kiss her. But he'd sure done it.

"Rumor has it there's a lot going on between you and Maisy." Brice entered Drake's office and took a seat across the desk.

Drake lifted his gaze from the computer screen. He did not welcome this conversation. The woman had not left his thoughts. "Rumors? So now you listen to gossip?"

Brice chuckled. "You know as well as I do that nobody in this town gossips. I take the truth as the truth."

Drake rolled his eyes and shook his head. "Right. I'm guessing you heard it from Aunt Trudy. Or Sally Ann or Gert? Those three are out of control. They are in a tizzy, as Gert would say."

Brice's eyes sparkled. "Tell me about it. I also heard it from Libby, Beth, and Jenna." He was ticking names off with his fingers. "Even saw Lori in town and she said she'd heard it too. And she and Trip have been out of town at a rodeo."

"Perfect," he growled.

"What'd you expect? Word on the street is someone saw you kissing her in the alleyway beside Gert's café. Seems like you two enjoy hanging out around the outside of the café. Were you looking for more skunks?" He chuckled, obviously tickled at his humor.

He deserved it; had brought it on himself. *He should not have kissed her. What had he been thinking?*

He was a grown man. A businessman. He'd always thought he was a fairly smart man but the moment she was near, he acted like a fool. Thus, the kiss. He dropped his forehead and rubbed his temple where a headache was building.

"She's really getting to you, isn't she?"

He glared at his brother. "You can tell she is. And you're enjoying this, aren't you?"

"Oh yeah. Big brother takes the fall. Wedding

bells will be ringing again before long."

"No, they won't."

"Everyone else is thinking the same as me. I don't think you can see the truth. You're going to fall hard. You've got it bad, brother."

"Don't you have something to do?" *Why was he even trying to deny it?* Ever since she'd gotten to town, he'd been distracted and everyone could see it.

Brice studied him hard. "You're supposed to have my cattle list for me. I head out early in the morning with the load to Amarillo. Remember?"

"Right. I...forgot." He went back to his computer, clicked a folder, and found what he was looking for and hit print. He could feel his brother's gaze watching him as he spun his chair around and grabbed the two pages the printer was spitting out.

"I never thought I'd see this day. You forgot." Brice grinned as he took the papers Drake handed to him across the desk.

"Don't get used to it. I'm a little distracted."

"You know it's okay. I'm glad to know you're human."

Drake could have told him that. Lately, he was forgetting all kinds of things. He had even opened the refrigerator and forgotten what he was looking for this morning when he'd gone across the ranch yard to the big house for a drink. It was true, Maisy Love had blown into his life like a tornado and was tearing him up.

He leveled his gaze at Brice. "Don't you have something better to do than come in here and bother me when I'm trying to work?"

Brice laughed again. "I came for this, remember?" He waved the papers.

Drake ground his teeth.

"Relax. I'm about to get out of your hair. Look, our cattle ranch has grown and our reputation is outstanding. A lot of that has to do with you, because of the focus and dedication you've given the business. You're practically a mastermind. You deserve some happiness, brother. Why don't you loosen up, see what happens? I know I'm teasing you because it's fun, but I really care for you—yeah, I know it's hard to believe. But I do. All of us have been hoping someone would come along and get your attention. But it's never happened. And then this pretty whirlwind blows in, and you can't think straight. Ask her out. See where it goes."

"Brice, I love you, man. But you're stepping into my business. I'm not asking her out."

"So you say. I've got five bucks that says you're going to. Remember the monthly street dance is coming up. Maybe if you can't get up the nerve to ask her out, you can ask her to dance. After the dance, you can walk away. Then again, maybe you won't be able to."

"Why do I feel like I'm a fish in a fishbowl right now?"

Brice stood. "Because you actually are." He laughed all the way out the door.

Drake shook his head. He stared back at the numbers on his computer screen and all he saw was Maisy's pretty face. And immediately he started thinking about that kiss again.

That kiss was going to be the death of him.

CHAPTER SEVEN

"Where did you go yesterday?" Sally Ann asked the next morning when Maisy went downstairs to fill her water bottle before going for her jog.

She'd anticipated the question. She was surprised to find Jenna there also.

"I heard there was a bit of excitement yesterday," Jenna said with interest as she took a sip of her coffee. "You gave Aunt Sally Ann and her cohorts a lot to twitter about."

"We weren't twittering. We just got excited at the

thought of a new romance. We didn't bother you, did we, Maisy? And from what I heard from Mary Monroe, who came into the diner a few minutes after you and Drake left, she saw Drake in the alley kissing a woman she didn't know. We figured that was you since you were the one who left with him." Excitement heightened her color. "Trudy was ecstatic at the news."

Everyone had been so nice to her. But this was way out of her realm. She was not used to people jumping into her business like this. Especially people she liked. But this was hard to take.

She caught Jenna watching her over the brim of her cup. "I know how you're feeling right now. They did this to me, and I was overwhelmed. Kind of like that skunk in a cage that brought you and Drake together. But, you can resist if you're not interested."

"You didn't resist much. You and Shane were meant for each other. All we did was egg you on a bit. Coffee, dear?" She held the pot up in offering to Maisy.

All Maisy wanted was to get out of there and get her jogging done and hopefully get some endorphins moving to help her mood. "No, but thanks for the offer. I'm after water." She moved to the farmhouse sink and filled it from the tap. She chose to level with these two. "This thing you think is between me and Drake won't work. He's not planning to marry. Did you know that? Not that this attraction between us means we're falling in love or anything. Way too premature for that. But, I just thought you should know so you don't get your hopes up. And besides that, I'm on the road all the time and have no plans to settle down for several years, if at all. I love my life. Marriage isn't meant for everyone."

Speculation in her expression, Sally Ann tapped her fingers on the coffee pot she still held. "Drake doesn't date a lot that any of us know about, but why would he not want to get married?"

Good question. One she had wondered about all night. Not that she was ready for that but it was curious to hear the *why* of his decision. It saddened her.

Jenna stood. "It is odd. And sad. But sometimes what we think we want turns out not to be what we really want. It just takes love to show up to become the key to open up new wants and dreams. At least that's what happened with me. Love changed my life in so many ways. But what is right for one might not be right for someone else. Anyway, Maisy, don't let my aunt railroad you into anything you're uncomfortable with."

"I wouldn't do something like that." Sally Ann picked up a cinnamon roll and bit into it.

Jenna huffed, "Um, right, like any of us believe that. Not to change the subject, but aren't you and Libby trying to figure out where to film her cooking segment?"

"Yes, we are," Maisy said, almost too quickly as relief filled her at not having to go into detail about her kissing Drake in the alley. That topic had somehow faded away as the conversation had turned to why Drake didn't want to marry. "I had thought about asking to do it here since the other visitors checked out yesterday. But I know Sally Ann has new reservations checking in today and I don't want to take up space. The diner is really busy. We could wait and do it on Sunday when Gert is closed but I'm hoping to do

Gert's show then if she's feeling like it."

Jenna beamed. "I think I have a solution. The kitchen at the big house at the ranch is large and beautiful and usually not that busy during the day because Marcus and the others are out working. I think it would be the perfect place. And I know Marcus wouldn't mind."

She hesitated. Drake worked at the ranch but she'd said everyone would be gone during the day. It would be okay. She wasn't ready to face Drake. Not yet. "If that's the case, that would be wonderful, if you think he wouldn't mind."

Jenna's eyes brightened. "I'll call right now and then I'll take you out there. Can you handle the shop while I do that?" she asked Sally Ann.

"I sure can. Take your time. I'll do it like I used to before you partnered with me. I'll put a note on the door, telling my boarders to come to the junk shop to check in. It worked before."

"Great. Hang on while I call Marcus. Shane actually suggested it when I was telling him the problem."

"That was nice of him to suggest it." Maisy drank some water and waited as Jenna walked into the other room and made the call.

"I'm still not giving up on the fact that when you and Drake are in the same room the tension rises. You know you like him. And then there is that kiss Mary saw. Maybe you should stick around longer. You don't even have to pay rent. Stay here as my guest. You're my friend now."

Wow, this struck Maisy hard that the B&B owner was so in hopes of romance happening between her and Drake that she would not want to charge the room rate. This was serious stuff. "Thanks for the generous offer but I couldn't do that. And I do have other places to be."

"What's the use of having this free lifestyle if you can't change up plans?"

"I have the freedom to change things up. But I've already had this trip disrupted. I need to go as soon as my Jeep is fixed, and the taping is done."

"But don't you love it here? Doesn't being on the road all the time get lonely?"

"I do love this town. And everyone has been so nice, if not a little pushy." She chuckled. "But I have goals." A detour in her plans had started to get complicated, but she was not giving in. Didn't matter anyway that she was attracted to strong, masculine Drake Presley. Didn't matter at all.

"It's all set." Jenna came into the room. "We can go anytime you're ready."

"Really," her jaw dropped. "I mean, great. Give me about thirty minutes to gather my equipment and I'll be ready to go check it out."

She hurried up the stairs and just hoped Drake wasn't around the ranch today. This was a perfect fix for her filming problem. But despite Jenna saying no one would be around the kitchen, she realized that might not mean she wouldn't run into Drake on the property.

The idea sent those irritating butterflies dipping in her stomach.

Problem was, it was with anticipation, not dread.

Drake was coming out of his office building on the end of the main barn when he spotted Jenna's car driving up the drive. He headed that way to see whether she was looking for Shane or whether she needed anything. He liked Jenna and had been thrilled that his brother had found someone who made him so happy. There had been moments when he'd thought things wouldn't work out between them. But somehow, they had and now his brother was sky-high with happiness. And he was happy for him, and all his brothers. Glad they'd been able to not be held captive by the past.

"Hey, Jenna," he greeted as he approached her parked car and she got out.

"Drake, you're here." She sounded more than a little startled.

"Yes, I'm working on the fall cattle sell register. Do you need—" His words halted as the passenger door opened and Maisy stepped out. She looked slightly uncomfortable but then she hid it behind a smile, that teasing light coming into her eyes.

He reacted instantly to the sight of her and his world blurred momentarily.

"Hello, Drake." Her gaze drank him in as much as he was drinking her in. "Jenna brought me out to use your dad's kitchen today. Libby will be out as soon as she gets off. Do you mind?"

She sounded as non-personal as someone he had just met on the street. Something inside his chest tightened. He fought to sound just as neutral but it wasn't easy when he found all he wanted to do was rush around the vehicle and take her in his arms and kiss her senseless again.

Man, he had it bad. His brother was right, and he'd known it all along.

"Hello, Maisy. I don't mind. Besides, this is Dad's place and he can do whatever he wants." The last words came out sounding snippy. Snippy did not suit him and did not make him happy.

She caught it and lifted one perfect eyebrow.

"Good to know," she said. "Jenna set this up, or I'd still be looking for a way to tape the segment with

Libby."

"That's right. I called Marcus after Shane put the idea in my head last night. He told me that everyone would be gone today, and Marcus said the same thing."

He knew that both his dad and Shane knew he was going to be here all day. The sale was a big deal and took a lot of time to coordinate. They had four big auction events each year, in between a few other smaller ones scattered through the year.

"It's fine. I'll stay out of y'alls way."

"You're always welcome to come bake with us." Maisy smiled mischievously.

His gut twisted with the vivid memory of how those lips had felt so warm and soft against his own. "No thank you. If you don't need anything, I'll head back to the office." He'd come for more coffee grounds for his office coffee pot but he could do without now. He forced himself to turn away.

"Drake," Jenna said in a rush. "Since you're here, could you help us carry Maisy's equipment inside?"

He turned back. "Sure. Be glad to."

"You don't have to," Maisy stated from over the

top of the car. "I'm used to doing this myself. No need to take up your time up."

Their gazes locked, and he saw the stubborn set of her jaw and that irksome challenge in her eyes. "I don't mind at all," he said, wanting to push her buttons for some fathomless reason. He strode to her side of the car where she remained rooted to the spot in front of the backseat passenger's door.

"You don't need to worry yourself about this," she muttered, looking spunky as a riled-up bunny rabbit.

"My mother taught me early to help a lady out and that's what I plan to do. If you'll move out of the way."

She didn't move. "I would think that your mother taught you to do it only if the lady in question wanted your help. I'm fine. Jenna was just being nice when she asked you. I'm very capable. I loaded it after all. Right, Jenna?"

He pulled his eyes off Maisy and saw Jenna looking very entertained as she studied them. Boy, would she have a story to tell. He wasn't sure what she was making out of his and Maisy's standoff but he could only imagine by the light in her eyes.

"Oh, you two are having far too much fun debating this. I'll stay out of it if you don't mind." She smiled and closed her door, then opened the passenger door on her side and pulled out a grocery bag. "I'll just take this into the kitchen. You two take your time."

"Now you've done it," Maisy hissed as Jenna disappeared through the front door. "Are you aware that someone saw you kissing me in that alley yesterday?"

"I'm afraid I am."

"Well, then let me tell you that you have now fueled an all-out matchmaking frenzy in your aunt and her buddies. They practically have us married despite me telling them you aren't marrying at all and I'm moving on as soon as I'm done here." She poked him in the chest again.

He wrapped his fingers around hers. "You're poking the bear again," he warned, focusing on her mouth and wanting more than anything to kiss her again.

"Don't you look at my lips. They are off-limits,

107

bucko. I'm not teasing you right now. I'm being dead serious. This is no laughing matter."

"No, it isn't." Then he chuckled, finding himself enjoying her dilemma and her riled-up state.

"Then why are you laughing?"

"Because you are about the cutest thing I've ever seen when you get riled up. It makes me want to kiss you."

"Well, don't." She backed up, but he held onto her hand. "This won't work for either of us."

"You're right, it won't. But that doesn't stop the fact that we are like flint and stone striking against each other."

She inhaled sharply. "Don't you get any ideas. No more kissing allowed."

He wasn't the type of man who would kiss a woman when she didn't want it. He'd lost his head yesterday in that alley and then she'd wrapped her arms around his neck and held on, so that pretty much said she was a willing partner in the kiss. But right now, she cocked her head to the side and leveled a warning.

"Stop thinking about kissing me. Stop it right now." Her eyes dropped to his lips and then she frowned. "Drat. Now you have me thinking about it and it's useless."

"Maybe not. You can't deny that it was pleasant."

She swallowed hard. "True, it was, and I'd be lying if I said anything else. But, we'd just be playing with fire to do it again. Especially since by next weekend, I'll be gone."

He was enjoying watching her squirm, and though he'd carried this further than he planned, this pushing her buttons, he was more tempted than he wanted to be about kissing her again. "Maybe your leaving is a good reason to kiss a few more times."

Her eyes widened and he was startled that he'd even suggested it. But he couldn't get her off his mind. And here she was...

Suddenly, she chuckled. "You're pulling my leg. Teasing me. It's a bad idea and you know it. So if you come on and help me carry this stuff inside, then you can go back to your ranch business and I can go back to my business."

She pulled her hand free and spun to open the car door. When she backed up to make room for the door to open, she rammed up against him and he had to fight not to wrap his arms around her and pull her against him. He backed up. He was playing with fire.

She pulled a box from the rear seat and rammed it into his arms. "Take this," she demanded, then dove back inside the car to pull out another box. "Lead the way, Mr. Hunky Man. This is what you asked to do and so I'm letting you. But there will be no hanky-panky to go along with it. Now move. I've got a show to produce."

He grinned. Man, the woman made him lighten up when she got all bossy and teasing. "Fine. But hanky-panky is really sounding good to me right now," he teased back.

But he meant every word.

CHAPTER EIGHT

"Just relax, Libby." Maisy hit the record button on the video cam she'd set up to film the cooking segment. Libby was more nervous than she'd figured. Libby was somewhat shy, but she hadn't anticipated that she'd be petrified.

But, oh boy, was she. Maisy looked at Jenna, who sat behind the camera, helping Maisy by working the record and off buttons. This was their third time to try to start the interview, so she was really coming in handy. On the camera, Libby looked as if she was ready to run far, far away. Jenna looked as worried as she was that Libby was either going to run or throw up.

"Take a deep breath. It's just us three in the room. And we're all friends."

Libby did as she was told and seemed slightly better.

"You can do this, Libby," Jenna encouraged.

"Thanks, I'm trying. It's just hard," Libby said hesitantly.

The fact that she'd managed to hold her ground and not run for the hills caused Maisy to be both grateful and impressed. She was determined to find a way to help Libby get comfortable with the camera and do what she loved. Because she did love baking pies; it showed in how delicious they were. Maisy could grow addicted to them, they were so light and fluffy and delicious. She'd thought she'd hit the jackpot in the wee hours of the morning when she'd found a pie in Sally Ann's icebox. She'd wandered down to the kitchen when she'd been unable to sleep and had gone in search of carbs and coffee. She ate two pieces before she'd forced herself to stop and go back to her room and pretend to sleep. Pretend, being all she could call laying there with her eyes closed, as thoughts of Drake and that amazing kiss swirled through her mind. She shook off the distracting thoughts and focused on Libby.

"Can you try just a little harder to relax?" she coaxed.

Libby nodded and smiled at the camera, looking about as stiff as a walking stick.

Maisy nodded at Jenna and she pressed the record button and nodded the go ahead.

"Hi, lovely viewers," Maisy greeted brightly. "I'm so glad you're here for a Maisy Love, On The Road cooking segment. And let me tell you, I have a very special guest today." She introduced Libby and met her frozen gaze, using her own to urge her to unfreeze. "I was lucky enough to discover Libby and the Goodnight Café in this small town of Ransom Creek after my vehicle broke down. It was very serendipitous since it got me at least two episodes for your enjoyment. We're doing pie today and next, Gert Goodnight is going to share her top-secret bread pudding recipe. So, stay tuned and don't miss an episode. But today, roll up your sleeves and let's grab ingredients and do some baking with Libby." She looked at Libby. "Why don't you tell everyone what kind of pie we're going to bake today?"

Libby continued to stare at the camera with the frozen smile on her face as if she had been blasted with dry ice. Maisy was going to have to just figure a way to edit the video before airing it.

"Libby, what are you going to bake today?" Maisy nudged her gently with her elbow and smiled her encouragement.

"We're going to bake my rubber, I mean my rhubarb-strawberry pie today," she said stiffly. But at least she'd spoken. And then the frozen smile returned, and she blinked several times, rapid-fire. It was not attractive in the video.

Maisy waved for Jenna to shut off the recording. There was no way to edit this. She turned to look at Libby and took her by the shoulders. "Girlfriend, you *have* to relax. I can't air that on the internet with you looking horrified. Petrified. And all the above. You need to look like you enjoy baking pies. Not like we're fixin' to chop you up and put you in one."

That made Libby smile sheepishly as she rubbed her forehead as if she were getting a headache. "I didn't know I was going to be like this. I mean, I'm trying, but that camera is intimidating. How do you do that all the time? I watched your videos last night and you're awesome. You could be on the cooking channel or something. You can have your own show—you're such a natural. And you make people so at ease. How do you do that?"

Maisy leveled skeptical eyes on the girl. "It's not working on you. So, I'm not exactly hitting the ball out of the park." She laughed. "Honestly, I simply try to help everyone know that it's a camera and it can't hurt you. And things can be edited. If you could just say hi then focus on your love of baking pies, soon you'll relax. Can you do that? You do enjoy baking pies, don't you?"

"I do." Libby stared at the camera for a brief instant, biting her lip. "I really do. Sometimes I just get really nervous. You should have seen all the plates I dropped when I first met Vance. It was terrible." She blushed.

"It's so true," Jenna agreed.

Maisy could envision it after seeing how petrified she'd been moments before. "Good to know. I'll put the pie in the oven just in case you decide to drop that. Then you can relax and just have fun, okay? My viewers are going to love you. Most of them are older women and will feel empathy for you being so nervous. You just need to get past being frozen in place. If you can do that, your pie is going to thrill them. They'll be able to gloat to their friends that they have the best rhubarb-strawberry pie recipe in all the state. You do know they do that, don't you?"

"They do?"

"Oh yeah. I get letters. Everybody tells me that theirs is the best—the best blackberry cobbler, peach dump cake, or chunky chocolate chip chocolate bars. Whatever it is, they do it the best. But they still watch my show to find new ideas. You can make them happy and teach them something because that pie is to die for—I had two pieces last night."

Libby looked a bit astounded. "Wow, thank you. You're passionate about this. I wasn't joking about you needing to be on TV. You should send a video to them."

Maisy had sent a video in a few months ago but nothing came of it. "I have," she admitted. "It's to compete against some other amateurs like me for fun and to maybe get some publicity for my program. But, I'm happy with what I do. Besides, me on television would probably give me a big head."

Libby smiled. "You're teasing, aren't you?"

She had been trying to relax Libby and was glad to see her teasing had helped. "I am. I'm pretty grounded and like to think nothing would go to my head. Are you ready to try this again?"

Libby nodded. "Okay, turn that thing back on and let's do this. I want to teach somebody something. I like the sound of that."

Feeling less stressed herself, Jenna turned the camera back on.

This had distracted her from thoughts of Drake

and she'd needed that. Boy did she ever after their encounter outside. All night and day, she'd had him and his kiss on her mind. And his challenge. Or a threat that if she teased him again, he might kiss her. She'd been so very tempted to say something to push his buttons because the overwhelming temptation to tease him, just to feel his kiss again, had slammed into her and was almost irresistible.

It was just that his kiss had been so, so stunning. It had been and there was no denying it. The man had swept her off her feet, made her feel things she'd actually wondered whether she was immune to. Evidently not.

Not indeed. And then he'd started pushing her buttons. It was as if he wanted to goad her into kissing him.

What had happened to the reserved cowboy she'd come to enjoy teasing so much before that amazing kiss?

She wasn't sure, and honestly, she was having to try to figure out what to do about the cowboy who'd taken his place.

Maisy was over there in the kitchen and he was having strange inclinations. Like the overwhelming thought of sneaking over there and peeking through the window to watch her in action. Instead, to fight the need, he pulled her web cooking channel up and watched her in action. She was so stinkin' cute, it shouldn't be legal. She lit up the screen and put her guests at ease so they could share their recipes with the world. He was going to get hooked on this channel. If he didn't watch out, he was going to get hooked on Maisy.

He was engrossed in watching her when his office door opened and his little brother walked in. "Vance," he said as he fumbled with clicking off the video he was watching and then jumped to his feet. "What are you doing here?"

"I live here." He laughed, eyeing him closely. "Is something wrong?"

"No, why?"

"You seem jittery."

Drake narrowed his gaze and fought to calm his thumping heart. Maisy was making him crazy. "I'm just surprised to see you."

"I came home a day early. Drove all night to get here. I'm looking for Libby. Gert said she was out here but that I shouldn't interrupt what's going on inside the house. She said Libby's baking pies for that internet show she told me about. I could hear her excitement about it when we were talking, but she was nervous too. You know how nervous she gets. I'm surprised she even agreed to it."

"I was too."

Vance looked worried. "Do you think it's going okay?"

Suddenly he had the excuse he needed to go sneak a peek through the kitchen window. "Let's go see. We can look through the window by the table."

Vance grinned widely. "Good idea. Let's go. I hope I can hold back. It's been hard being on the road these last few weeks and having to leave Libby behind. I don't know if I can keep doing it."

"But you're on track again to win the NFR. These

shots you're getting aren't going to keep coming forever. You need to focus and hang in there."

Vance looked troubled. "I know. And I have a plan. I just need to see Libby."

They strode across the gravel parking area between the barns and the house. When they reached the house, they skirted around to the back and eased up to the window. From this angle, they had a view of the kitchen area. Jenna was sitting on a stool beside the camera in a tripod and big light reflectors on either side of her that faced toward Maisy and Libby.

"She's so beautiful," Vance breathed, grabbing the window ledge.

Drake was staring at Maisy and though he knew Vance was talking about Libby, he was thinking how pretty and vibrant Maisy was. The woman glowed as she talked to the camera and then teased Libby enough to make her smile as she stirred something on the stove.

"Drake, I can't take it. I still have three months to go to get as high as I can in the rankings going into the NFR and I can't take being away from Libby."

Drake frowned. Vance's dream and passion had always been to win the bronc riding at the National Finals Rodeo. And he'd been close but missed both years. This was his year; he'd been so on target all year that it was amazing. And then he'd met Libby and his timing had gone to the dogs. They'd all seen it. Still, he spoke with caution, "I thought y'all had agreed to wait until after the finals was the best thing."

"We did," Vance whispered, his eyes glued on Libby. "But you've seen my scores. I'm off. Off bad. I can't concentrate. I can't think of anything but Libby. I'm ready to throw in the towel and come home. But I know Libby wants to come with me but I won't do that unless she's my wife. So, I've come home to ask Libby to marry me now—this weekend—and come on the road with me." He stared back through the window and sighed. "I love her, Drake, and I just can't stand being away from her."

His words touched Drake. He put his hand on his little brother's shoulder. He wished only good things for Vance. He was tough, competitive, and a really nice guy. He deserved every good thing that life had because he worked hard to achieve his goals and never lost sight of being humble and kind.

"Then ask her. Because I know she misses you too. She talks about you all the time and she needs to be happy too. Now, we better stop snooping and wait on the porch for them to finish. You can tell me what your plans are and I'll do whatever I can to help you get it done."

"Thanks. I knew you would. I called Dad and told him. He was glad too. Is he home?"

"Nope, he helped with the loading at daylight, before Brice set out for Amarillo with another load of cattle. Then, I'm not sure where he headed off to but I suspect maybe to try to see Karla. He wasn't here when I arrived." His dad was a grown man and didn't always answer to them about where he was heading off to. He'd been spending more time away from the ranch over the past several months, spending time with Karla when she was off.

"He was distracted when I talked to him. I even think he sounds stressed out. Is he feeling okay? I mean, is his heart doing okay? I worry about him since the heart attack."

Drake inhaled deeply. He still had a hard time thinking that his dad, as fit-looking as he was, had had a heart attack in his fifties. "Yeah, me too. He takes care of himself and Karla keeps an eye on him too. Her being a nurse, she's pretty watchful. He follows his diet. Maybe he and Karla had a fight or something." That was almost a joke. She adored his dad. He wasn't exactly sure how his dad felt though.

"Maybe. Anyway, I'm sure I'll catch him in the morning when we both meet in the kitchen for coffee at daylight."

None of the Presley men slept late. Chores at the ranch started early, so Drake knew Vance would see his dad in the morning. They went around to the front of the house and were leaning against the wide cedar porch columns thirty minutes later when the ladies came out of the door. They were talking excitedly but all talking stopped the instant Libby spotted Vance. She squealed and threw herself across the porch and into his waiting arms.

"Vance, you're home. Why didn't you tell me you

were coming in early?" she rambled as she hugged him fiercely.

Vance bent around her, almost absorbing her, he was holding her so tightly. "I couldn't stand not seeing you another day. Come on. I need to talk to you about something important." He didn't even look at anyone else as he led Libby away, around the house and toward the backyard.

Drake knew they would go to the swing that had been kept perfect all these years. The swing that had been his mother's favorite spot. His father had given it to her as a Valentine's gift one year, and she'd loved it dearly. She'd spent hours there swinging all the boys and spending time watching sunsets with his dad. Drake swallowed a hard lump in his throat thinking about how much his dad and mom had loved each other.

Why wasn't Vance or Cooper or Shane worried about how they'd feel if they lost Libby or Beth or Jenna?

He frowned, the question reverberating through him like thunder.

"What are y'all doing out here?" Jenna asked.

Jolted, he tried not to appear shaken. "We were waiting on Libby. Vance has something important to discuss with her." He looked at Maisy and found her watching him. "How did it go with the filming?"

"We nailed it finally. She did great. And I got to eat an *amazing* piece of pie. Just so you know, there are one and a half pies in the refrigerator for all of you fellas. There would have been two pies, but us three girls ate half of one. They're delicious. She has a special skill with crust and meringue." She laughed. "She just has a skill when it comes to pies, period."

"Yes, she does," Jenna agreed. "I'm taking a piece home for Shane. He'll thank me. Sadly, baking is not my specialty but the sweet man doesn't seem to mind. And I have all these friends and my aunt who do it so well, I can just use their talent." She laughed. "Works for me."

"Shane probably agrees, so you're okay." Drake smiled from her to Maisy and immediately wasn't thinking about pie. "If you're ready to take all that down, I'll help."

Jenna looked relieved. "That would be great. Aunt Sally Ann texted me that a bus of ladies just arrived and she's swamped. I feel bad leaving Maisy alone."

"Then you two go ahead and head into town. I'll load this up and run it into town when I'm done."

Maisy shook her head. "You go ahead and go, Jenna. You were a lifesaver today. Couldn't have done it without you, but I'll help gather the equipment then let Drake be my chauffeur into town."

He was surprised that she was planning to ride with him. "I'd be happy to." *More than happy.*

"Wonderful. Thanks so much." Jenna didn't wait for him to change his mind; instead, she was backing toward her car as she spoke. "You two behave." She winked, opened her car door and almost dove inside. She slammed her door and gunned the motor in her haste to start the car and back out.

Drake had to wonder by her rush to get out of there so fast whether Sally Ann really needed her so desperately or whether she was jumping on the matchmaking bandwagon with his aunt, her aunt, and Gert. He wouldn't put anything past this female crew.

Maisy turned to him, shock on her face. "Boy, she almost dove for her car to get out of here. I think she didn't want me changing my mind."

"She was in a hurry." He found he couldn't help smiling at her.

Her lip twitched. "I declare, Drake Presely, you are smiling. Better be careful or folks will get the idea you're no longer the serious one."

He laughed. "Can't have that. I'll get myself straightened out before we reach town."

Bright eyes dug into him, reaching places he tried hard to keep hidden away.

"That would probably be best. If the ladies think you've softened, you'll be a target for sure where their meddling is concerned."

"And that would not be good." He could stand here and talk to her all day. Who was he trying to kid, he could stare at her all day. "How did your taping go?"

"Shaky at first. Libby was so nervous. I had no idea she was that camera shy. But we made it and her segment will be great after I get it edited. Jenna was a huge help."

He leaned a shoulder against the porch post and crossed his arms. "You're really good at what you do."

She cocked her head and her lips twitched. "How do you know? Maybe because you were peeking through the window?"

"You saw?"

"I did, but I had to keep a straight face. I didn't see Vance though. He wasn't in my line of sight. I have to admit I was sure curious about what Mr. Serious was doing watching me through the window?"

"Sorry about that. Vance needed to see Libby. He hasn't seen her in a couple of weeks and he's madly in love."

"I got that. And she's the same." They stared at each other. "Well, we better load this stuff and I'll get out of your hair."

"Right. Lead the way."

She spun and headed back into the house, her curved hips swaying gently as she hurried down the entrance hall.

"Do you have eyes in the back of your head? I

figure that's the only way you saw me in that window earlier."

She laughed. "I do, so now you know. Eyes up, cowboy."

He stopped watching those nicely swaying hips and chuckled. *Maybe she really could see him.*

They entered the kitchen, and she indicated a box. "If you'll take that one, I'll carry this one."

"Whoa, not so fast. Didn't you say there was pie in there?" He nodded toward the refrigerator.

"There is, and it's delicious."

"You can't tell a man that and then expect him to not want a piece. Do you have time to wait?"

"Sure." She was closest to the refrigerator, so she reached to open the door just as he moved to take hold of the door handle. "I've got this," she said, her shimmery lavender eyes catching his and holding. "Grab a plate."

He hesitated, realizing this might not have been the brightest idea on his part. It wasn't pie he wanted but to hold her again. To kiss her, and feel her reaction to him as she'd done in the alley. "Right." He sidestepped her and took a plate from the cabinet. "Want one?"

"Oh no, that would be far too much pie for me in one day. I'll just have to watch you enjoy it."

She placed the pie on the counter and their arms brushed against each other as she unwrapped the plastic wrap from the golden-crusted pie. A burst of pleasure shot through him and he moved closer so there was more contact. He could not deny that she drew him. He'd been trying to deny it ever since she'd arrived in Ransom Creek. He was playing with fire and he knew it.

She had grabbed a pie cutter from the jar of utensils on the counter and had a giant portion sliced in seconds. When she looked up at him, he could see in her eyes that his nearness was having an effect on her too. He was so tempted to kiss her. She was irresistible to him.

Her hand to his chest stopped him when he had shifted toward her. "Don't," she said. "I haven't teased you." Her words were soft. She reached for the plate and handed it to him.

He looked from her lips to the pie. "Right." He took it and turned to the large island in the kitchen and pulled out a barstool. He was losing it. He needed to get hold of himself.

She placed a fork on his plate. "You'll need that. But I can verify that it is edible with only your fingers. I held the slice in my hand in the wee hours this morning."

She pulled out a chair next to him and he wondered why she was choosing to be so close instead of putting space between them. It would have made things easier at this point.

Instead of dwelling on it too much, he ate a generous fork full of the berry pie. It was a beautiful red pink tone and melted in his mouth with an explosion of tangy sweetness. The crust flaked and crumbled with it and the texture was amazing.

"You like it, don't you?" She leaned her chin in her cupped hands and smiled warmly at him.

His insides warmed accordingly. "Yes, I do." And he wasn't just talking about the pie. "She outdid herself on this. Vance is going to gain weight. No way can he resist these if she bakes them all the time."

"He'll enjoy himself, though." Her eyes twinkled.

He almost sighed looking at her. "Yeah, for certain. I am." And then, unable or unwilling to stop himself, he leaned over and kissed her.

A small gasp burst from her lips as he brushed his against hers. He dropped his fork and spun his stool slightly so he was facing her as he reached around her and urged her closer. She slid from her barstool to nestle between his thighs. Her hand rested on his chest as her lips joined his in a warm and willing kiss. He'd never experienced anything like this, craving the feel of her, the touch of her. The taste of her. He hadn't meant to kiss her. He wasn't a man who lost control. Never had been. Until now. He groaned and wrapped both arms around her. Sliding his hand into the thick mass of dark hair, he tugged her closer. He couldn't seem to get close enough to her.

Wasn't sure he ever could.

CHAPTER NINE

Maisy's world swam around her. She'd known she was pushing the limits on the attraction spiking between them when she'd sat on the stool so close to Drake. But she'd ignored the danger, danger of escalating the temptation to feel his lips tangled with hers again. It was just too overwhelmingly strong a need. *A need.*

Yes, she'd *needed* to feel this. To feel her hands in his hair and his kiss rocking her world. Something about him was just too much for her to deny.

Breathing hard, she deepened the kiss, tasted the

delicious pie and found him even more irresistible. She'd never, ever eat pie again without thinking of this kiss. She settled closer against him and felt joy when he groaned softly against her lips. His heart pounded against hers. He smelled of man and sun and leather and that delicious cologne she'd be tempted to buy and carry with her for the rest of her life. A reminder of the man who'd worn it.

"Oh." A gasp behind them had them yanking apart to find a startled Libby and a widely grinning Vance standing behind her, studying them. "I'm sorry, I, we didn't mean to interrupt." Libby spun to run but Vance blocked her way and he wasn't budging.

"You two go right along and enjoy yourselves." He wrapped his arms around Libby. "Don't mind us."

Maisy was mortified. She stuttered breathlessly, "W-we were just…enjoying a piece of pie."

Vance chuckled. "I can see that. Libby's pies have that same effect on me." He kissed Libby's forehead and then placed his arm over her shoulders so that she had to turn back to them. Libby's eyes were bright.

"So sorry we interrupted," she said again.

"It's fine." Drake finally spoke. His hand rested possessively on her shoulder as he gently squeezed.

Was that to reassure her? He didn't have to protect her. She was a grown woman and if she wanted to kiss someone, him included, then she could. If he'd only known how much she'd enjoyed kissing him.

"It is. I'm going to look forward to your pies even more now that I know their secret powers." Maisy laughed and then moved away from Drake, needing space to gather her brains again. She moved to the pie and started covering it with the cellophane again. "Did you two have a good reunion?"

"Yes," Libby said, and something in her voice pulled Maisy to look at the woman. Excitement pinked her cheeks. "We're getting married. In three days."

"Congratulations." Drake moved across the room to slap his brother on the shoulder and to give Libby a gentle kiss on the cheek.

Maisy watched, delight ringing through her for the tenderness he showed Libby, and for her and Vance herself. "This is wonderful." She gave Libby a hug and patted Vance's arm. She barely knew him and it would have been awkward giving him a hug.

He grinned proudly. "Thanks. She's going on the last leg of the run for the NFR with me. We had agreed to wait until after the championship but I need her with me. It just doesn't feel the same out there by myself with her being back here waiting."

"And I want to. I just didn't want to get in his way." Libby looked at him with adoration and love in her eyes.

He kissed her nose and kept his forehead against hers. "You'll never be in my way."

Maisy's heart did a flip-flop, imagining Drake saying that to her. Imagining her saying it to him. The very idea stunned her speechless for a moment. *Was she falling in love with Drake?*

That moment, the room suddenly filled up as Marcus Presley walked in, followed by two of his other sons, Cooper and Shane.

"Hi, everyone," Marcus said. "Vance, where did you come from, son?" He took in the four of them with welcoming eyes then moved forward and gave his youngest son a hug, Cooper and Shane greeted them all, and she and Drake and Libby greeted them. It was a bit chaotic for a moment.

They were covered in a fine layer of dust, making it apparent that they'd been doing some kind of ranch work. She remembered Drake saying that Brice was hauling cattle to Amarillo. But other than him or their sister Lana being here, this was the most of them she'd seen in one room. She had met Cooper and Shane that first day but hadn't run into them again. And she hadn't met Marcus, but it was apparent who he was. He was an older version of Drake. The man had those emerald green eyes that each of his sons had in varying degrees of vivid wonder. They were gorgeous, like the varying colors of light deflecting off the sparkling jewel tones.

She was aware that Drake had moved closer to her as everyone moved into the room and she felt his hand brush hers. Felt the shimmer of awareness race through her and had to force herself not to shift closer to him.

"I'm glad you're all here," Vance said, his voice steady. "Libby and I are getting married in three days. We're heading into town first thing in the morning to get our marriage license and on Sunday afternoon, we're going to have the preacher marry us beside Mom's swing."

"Well, it's about time." Cooper slapped him on the shoulder. "I've been wondering how you were holding out."

Shane grinned. "Me and Jenna wondered too. We couldn't put ours off for months. We wanted to be married as soon as possible."

Libby blushed profusely. "We did too. But Vance was so busy."

"She insisted on not getting in my way and I tried to go with what she said she wanted, but I just can't do it. I talked her into moving it up. Coming with me and making this run for the win something we do together."

Maisy loved it. He was so sweet, the way he wanted to include Libby in his life's goals and dreams. She thought about that. *What would it be like to share her goals and dreams with someone? To not travel alone, or not to think as one but as a unit?*

She was still thinking about that twenty minutes

later when Drake drove up to the B&B. It had grown dusky, with a faint glow of daylight shimmering before it gave over to darkness. It was quiet as they climbed from the truck. There were a couple of vehicles parked on the curb, probably the new guests. And the lights glowed in all the rooms. Her mouth was dry as she and Drake met at the back bumper to get her supplies out of the truck's bed.

"Thanks for the ride."

"My pleasure." He lowered the tailgate, and they both reached for the same box. Their hands brushed again. It was as if they were drawn together by a magnet and they kept brushing together again and again.

She pulled back. "I'm really happy for Libby and Vance."

"Me too. I'm enjoying seeing my little brothers and my sister happy and content."

She studied him. "That's what I don't understand. You are happy to see them getting married, so you're not anti-marriage for everyone?"

"No," he sighed. His hands rested on the top edges

of the box with her equipment in it. He stared toward the back of Sally Ann's property and then met her gaze. There was such pain and need and…longing there.

"Does this come from losing your mom? Or someone else you once loved?" She touched his hand, needing to comfort him.

"My mother. I was old enough to see everyone's pain and to feel my own clearly. I know and remember how horrible it felt, how it still aches. Her leaving us left a gaping hole that took us all years to accept and heal from. I healed by trying to ease everyone else's pain—my younger siblings' and my dad's. I don't ever want to have something that terrible to happen to me again. Or to my family, if I were to give in and have one. I can only prevent that from happening if I vow never to marry."

His admission deeply saddened her. "You're denying yourself happiness just to ward off the possibility of sorrow?"

He looked thoughtful. "You could say that."

"Wow." She turned her back to the tailgate and

relaxed her hips against it as his words sank in. "I wasn't expecting that. You seem like someone who wouldn't let the past control you."

"What does that mean? I'm not. I'm taking control of my future with the choices I make, because of my past."

She cocked her head toward him. "Not the way I see it."

They stared at each other, almost in challenge.

"What about you? What's your story? Why are you so bound and determined to not let anyone into your life?"

"I never said that."

"Yeah, you did. You've got places to be and see, and you're seeing and doing it alone. No plans to slow down. That's not letting anyone into your life. Does it have something to do with your dad dying and your mother's actions since his death?"

She inhaled sharply. He was looking into her soul, it seemed. *Were they the same?* "Maybe...I don't want to lose anyone else I love or might love. My mother got over my dad so quickly. I didn't—haven't. I've lived the last three years hurting and missing him and I don't see it getting any easier in the near future. I couldn't bear it if I let someone else into my life and they died. I couldn't take it. I'm strong but not that strong. So staying unattached is easier. Safer."

He startled her when he traced a finger along her face, pushing her hair back tenderly. "I'm sorry for your loss."

A lump formed in her throat near her collarbone. It ached violently as she looked at him. "Thank you."

"Your pain is newer than mine. Rawer. And I can't explain your mother's actions but maybe this is her way of coping. Have you ever asked her? My dad coped by drawing into himself and feeding all his effort into us and the ranch. I coped by becoming a stable brother to my brothers and sister. Someone they could always count on. And they've all coped in varying ways. You've found your way of coping on the road and keeping mobile. Never slowing down for long. You're a rolling stone that catches no moss."

His words hit home. The cowboy was wise. "Maybe I am. And, as to my mom, I've never asked her," she murmured. "But one man after the other isn't right no matter how much she could have been hurting."

"I didn't say it was right. Maybe it's the only way she's found to fill the hole your dad left in her life. Or to temporarily fill the void in her heart."

Could it be? Had she been so hurt by her mother's actions that she'd just let her anger build walls between them so that they couldn't talk about the real issues?

"You might be onto something with that." She managed a smile at him.

"I hope you come to find peace about it. Maybe reach out and ask her."

"I don't know if I can."

He tilted her chin up and her pulse went crazy with the look in his eyes and the touch of his fingers. "Maisy Love, I believe you can do anything you set your mind to."

His words seeped into the dark corners of her soul like balm. No one had encouraged her like this since her father. He'd been her number-one cheerleader when it came to going after her dreams. Her mother had always been more reserved, more of the take the safe route. It suddenly hit her that maybe in finding one relationship after the other that her mother might be taking the safe route. *Was she afraid to be alone?*

And was Maisy afraid not to be alone?

"I need to go. Thanks again for bringing me home. I mean, back to the B&B."

"Are you going to come to the wedding? Libby wants you there."

Libby had asked her in very heartfelt words to come to the private ceremony. The ceremony that was going to delay her leaving, considering she and Gert would have to put off their baking session. But it was for a good cause. "Yes, I can't refuse such a wonderful invitation. I'm not family but I'm touched and will be there."

"Good. Can I pick you up? Take you?"

Was he asking her on a date, to the wedding? "Um, I could ride with Gert or Sally Ann."

"I know. But I'm asking if you'd go with me?"

The world spun a little, and she felt as if they were

standing on the edge of a cliff. They could stand on solid ground or they could step out in…faith, in hope? In a test to at least see where this could go.

"Okay." She couldn't get anything else out. *Had she just made a huge mistake?*

"Good." And then he leaned in and kissed her lips—soft, quick, and with the promise of more to come.

She stood frozen as she watched him carry the box toward the back porch. Her insides were mush as she picked up the smaller box and followed him on unsteady legs. *This was ridiculous. Why was a brush of his lips affecting her like this? Why was she feeling as if something momentous had happened to her in the last two days?*

She walked slowly up the steps, her pulse racing. *Would he kiss her again? Would she grab him and kiss him again?*

No, you will not.

He had set the box on the pretty table overlooking the backyard and reached for her box. Their hands brushed once more as his intense eyes met hers, dove into hers, before taking the full weight of the box and setting it on the table. Neither of the boxes weighed very much. Her equipment was small and the light reflectors were larger but weightless. It could all fit in a single box but she didn't like crowding things. They both knew his helping her was just a matter of him being taught to be a gentleman. And she assumed by his kisses and the look in his eyes that he wanted to spend time with her.

"I can take it from here," she said. "I don't want to disturb Sally Ann's guests. I'm going to scoot up the back staircase to my room." She had things to think about. And video to edit. And more things to think about…kisses to re-live.

"Then I'll head out." He moved past her and she watched him walk down the two steps to the brick pavers that made the sidewalk.

She tried to come up with some quirky goodnight but nothing was firing quick enough in her brain at the moment.

He tipped his hat and his lip hitched slightly upward. "Goodnight. Sleep well."

"You too," was all she could come up with. She was losing her edge. And as she watched him stride into the darkness, she knew sleeping well was not in her immediate future.

CHAPTER TEN

Drake didn't sleep. Instead, he headed out to the barn to saddle his horse. He planned to go for a ride but as he rounded the gate that would let him out into the pasture he spotted a man's shadow. He slowed his horse. *Who was on the property this late at night?*

"Drake." His father's voice was unexpected.

He halted his horse. "Dad, what are you doing?"

"Thinking."

In the moon's light, he could see the strain on his dad's features. His dad wasn't one to show a lot of strain. He was a master of hiding his emotions but

Drake knew he'd heard his dad weep in those early days after his mother died. Watched him walk or ride off for solitude and though he'd not been that old, Drake had known that was what he did when he needed to gather his wits and come back strong for his kids. It had been a long time since he'd seen this strain on his dad's face. Immediately, he dismounted.

"It's late and from the tension of your expression, something is wrong. Are you feeling okay? Is it your heart?"

Marcus wasn't wearing his hat, and the moonlight caught the few gray strands of hair at his temple and shimmered, reminding Drake that his dad was getting older. It was an inconceivable thought to him. This was the man he looked up to above all else, and he saw him as invincible. But, he knew time didn't stop marching for anyone.

"It's not my heart. Not in that way, anyway. Karla broke it off with me. Told me she didn't want to date any longer."

"What? Really?" He couldn't believe it. Karla was crazy for his dad. Had been almost from the moment

Marcus became her patient after heart surgery. She was the best. And had been the first woman his dad had shown interest in after all the years since losing his wife. "She's crazy for you." He repeated his thoughts. "What happened?"

"I don't know. She's been different this last couple of months. Quieter, more subdued. I have asked her over and over what's wrong, but that just seemed to make her withdraw more. I haven't said anything about it because I kept thinking she would change her mind. But I've been worried, not knowing what I'd done to change things between us. And now, tonight before I came home, she broke it off with me. Without explanation."

"But when you came into the house earlier, you looked fine." *Hadn't he?* There had been so much going on, with him being distracted by kissing Maisy and then Vance and Libby, and then his dad and his brothers entering the scene. *Had he really looked closely at his dad? No.* But he'd been smiling and happy for Vance and Libby.

But he was the master of hiding his emotions in

front of his family. It was typical.

"I didn't want to worry anyone, especially with Vance and Libby announcing they were getting married. And I don't want you saying anything either. I don't want to detract from their happiness at all."

"I get that. You were always there for us. You have never wanted to cause any of us pain. But, Dad, you're important to us and we want to be there for you too."

Marcus let out an audible sigh. "It's not that easy a thing to do. After your mom died, all of you were so hurt and mourning and I got used to closing off my needs. I don't talk about them much. It's just the way I am. You're that way too, you know."

He was. He knew it. "Maybe so. Did you open up to Karla much? Let her in on that part of yourself you keep hidden from all of us?"

In answer, his dad turned and strode to the pipe fence. He wrapped his hands around the middle rail and just stood there, staring out into the shadows. He looked like a man trying to hold up a wall. A wall that he'd built around himself.

Drake moved to stand beside him. He had the uncomfortable feeling that he was doing the same thing his dad seemed to be doing. *But you let Maisy in. You opened up to her about some of your feelings from those days of loss and pain.* It was true; he had.

"No, I didn't talk to her about the past. Not much anyway."

"Did she ask about it?"

"Yes, but she finally stopped when she realized I didn't want to talk about it. Didn't want to open up old wounds."

Drake stared out across the dark pasture, his thoughts churning. "When did she stop asking?"

He felt his dad turn to stare at him. "I don't remember. A while ago. I was just glad she finally stopped and we could just have a good time together."

"When, Dad? It may be important. Something tells me it's really important."

Marcus raked a hand through his hair. "A few months ago. We argued a little. And I made it clear to her that it wasn't something I wanted to talk about."

"You closed her out. I bet it was then that she

153

started being quieter."

His dad's jaw tensed and he cleared his throat after a moment. "Yes. You're right."

"Dad, do you just care for Karla as someone to have dinner with?"

"No. You know she's the first woman since your mom that I…"

"That you've loved?"

"Maybe. Yes. But that's not something I can get my emotions around. It's tough."

Drake understood in some ways. The emotional scars he carried were similar and yet not as deep as his dad would feel them. His dad would feel them from another perspective, one Drake never wanted to experience. And yet he knew in that moment that his dad needed to let go. "Maybe it's time you opened up to Karla. It seems to me that she needed you to open up to her."

"But I don't want to."

Drake bit the bullet. "I think from everything I've ever heard about love, that it's not always about you, but about what each of you needs. That sometimes you have to give the one you love what they need."

Marcus's features drooped. "And you think that's what she was asking me for, because she needed…"

"Needed to be included in all of your life, or into your heart. Maybe you were holding out on her? I mean, does she know you love her?"

"No, I haven't been able to let myself say the words. I can't."

Drake took in his dad's words. Heard the deeper hurt, the scars. The fear. "Yeah, I get that, Dad."

"The problem is, I wasn't ready to lose her either."

"Then maybe you need to let go. Move forward, you know?"

They stood there in silence, Drake taking his words in just as deeply as his dad seemed to be taking them.

"Thanks, son." Marcus said at last then turned the tables on him and asked, "How are you doing? I'm hearing things about you and Maisy. And you are very similar to me in that you're out here in the middle of the night too."

His jaw tightened. "She's on my mind." He

considered that statement. It wasn't anywhere near the true measure of how much she was dominating his thoughts. "I've never met anyone like her."

"You care for her?"

"I've just met her. Barely know her."

His dad gave a knowing laugh. "That doesn't really matter. Do you know, the first time I saw your mother was all it took and I couldn't help falling in love. I was at a rodeo and in the arena when she walked up onto the catwalk. She stunned me. I was just standing there in the pen with a bull I had just ridden and I should have been running for my life, getting the heck out of that pen. Instead, I was standing there, staring at her. And she was staring at me. I found out later it was because the bull was charging at me from behind. When I woke, laying on a stretcher, before they took me to the hospital, she was standing off to the side with a group of the waiting bull riders. I lifted my head from the stretcher and grinned like a fool at her. I proceeded to tell her I was going to marry her." He laughed. "I didn't even know her name."

Drake was stunned. His dad had never shared this

story with him. Maybe with no one. It was so out of character for his quiet, introspective dad. His heart stumbled over itself as he stared at his dad. This man he obviously didn't know as well as he thought he did.

"Yeah, clearly out of character for me. I loved your mother from the first moment I met her. It wasn't just that she was pretty. She wasn't the prettiest female in the room, but she was the most beautiful woman I've ever seen in my life. Something about her called to me, and her eyes reached out to me and seemed to speak to me."

Drake nearly choked up. "Wow, Dad. That's a story."

"Yeah, it's not something I share. It's my memory." He blinked hard and returned his gaze to the darkness. "I couldn't have *not* fallen in love with her. I had no choice and to this day, despite having had her in my life far too short a time, I don't regret a moment I spent with her."

Drake was trying to process all his dad had just revealed. It was overwhelming. But he had heard the despair in his dad's voice; he reached a hand to grasp his shoulder, trying to comfort him, not sure what words to speak. "I guess it is hard to love again after loving like that?"

"It's not something you can let go of. I don't want to."

Drake had no words for that. He felt sad for Karla. "I understand. I'm sure Karla sensed that and realized she couldn't compete with Mom or her memory." The realization just came to him as he was speaking. It had probably hurt her to her very core.

"Yeah. I'm sure she did. Now I just have to let her go. It's not fair to her for me to try to hold onto her."

"Right. You can't help how you feel." His dad was quiet and Drake couldn't help thinking he looked like a man who'd just been dealt terrible news. He was sad for his dad and for Karla. "Well, I'll leave you alone and let you work through this."

"Drake, I don't know what's holding you back from looking for a meaningful relationship. Or trying to find the woman who will be your soulmate. But remember, I wouldn't give up a moment of my time with your mother."

"Thanks, Dad. I think I'll ride a bit."

He mounted again and his dad opened the gate and watched him ride through. Drake tipped his hat and then nudged his horse into a lope. He couldn't get his dad's words out of his mind.

"What do you mean it's going to take a little longer?" Maisy stood in the middle of the mechanic's shop and stared at the man. "You said a week. I'm hoping to leave Tuesday morning." Right after she and Gert taped the show, in the kitchen while the diner was open. Hoss and whoever Gert found to take Libby's place would have to take care of everything. She just hoped Gert could find someone to take Libby's place on such short notice because she and Vance would already be on their way to his next rodeo.

If that wasn't already enough of a complication, now she was learning that there was more wrong with her vehicle than the mechanic had realized. More than he could fix.

"I ordered the part I need, but it's back ordered.

Unfortunately, it's got to make the long journey from Canada. And it's stuck at customs for some reason.

"I can't help it if you have a vehicle with hard to find parts they don't make anymore. This is the only part I can find and I'm lucky to find that."

Calm down. He's right. "I'm sorry. I just can't believe it myself." That meant, other than renting a car and leaving town then coming back for the Jeep later, she was stuck here. For at least another week. "Okay, I guess, then, let me know when you know more. Thank you."

"Will do." He scratched his head just above his left ear, leaving a grease spot on his skin since his hair had been shaved to the scalp. "I heard you and Drake might be tying the knot."

Shock hit her like a tidal wave. "No," she gasped. "That's Vance and Libby. Tomorrow."

He frowned and scratched his head again.

Did the man have fleas from the hound dog who lay snoring in the corner?

"Nope. I heard you and Drake. I know the difference between the eldest and the youngest brother.

Why would you want to leave if you're gettin' married?"

"I'm not getting married." *Where did things like this come from?*

He looked as if he didn't believe her. Or really, more as if he didn't think she knew what she was talking about and she was the one supposedly getting married.

Dear Lord, give me patience.

"I'm not getting married and I hope you'll not spread rumors."

"Well, don't go gettin' all huffy about it. Seems like you'd be excited or happy."

She frowned. "About what?"

"Gettin' married."

She scratched her head. Maybe she should have found another mechanic because this one was worrying her. But there wasn't another one in town.

She spun and stomped out of the garage, baffled but opting to just walk away for now. She stalked across the vacant lot toward the diner. The skunk was gone, and so far, no one had reported seeing any new ones around, therefore she assumed it was safe now. Still, when she made it to the alley and headed toward the front of the building, she was relieved. When she reached the kissing spot, she paused, overcome with the moment Drake had taken control and kissed her senseless.

And changed her life.

Prior to that moment, she'd still been in control of her life. But now, she felt out of control. And she was floundering.

Her mouth went dry, and she hurried forward, almost desperate to get away from the spot. Not sure what to do with herself, she headed down the street and then crossed it to walk to Sally Ann's junk shop, Junk to Treasure. She'd only been inside a couple of times to see Sally Ann or Jenna, but the shop intrigued her. She loved older things and it was so large one could get lost in there exploring. Maybe that was what she needed, to explore and not think for a while. She walked into what looked like a meeting of all the Presley women.

"Oh, hey," she said. Cooper's wife, Beth, was

there, and Jenna, along with two other women she didn't know.

"Hi, Maisy, you're just in time," Jenna greeted her with a welcoming smile. "Come in and meet Bella and Lori. Bella is married to Shane's and the guys' cousin, Carson. And Lori is one of their longtime friends and owner of the Calhoun Ranch next door, along with her husband, Trip, who is also an old friend of the fellas. We're cooking up a special surprise for Libby for tonight. A bachelorette party."

"Oh, she'll love that. And hello." She looked at Bella and Lori and they all greeted one another.

"We hope so," Bella added. "This has all been sped up since we were expecting it in four months instead of now. But we can handle it."

"Yes, we can." Lori yanked a thumb at Bella. "She can. She's the professional party planner and in charge. I can plan to get rodeo stock to and from a rodeo—but a party? Not my thing. But I can be told what to do and where to be and I'm willing." She laughed. "It's nice to meet you. Anyone who is a friend of Drake's is a friend of mine. I love that guy."

Maisy stalled on her words and the happy look in Lori's expression. She looked around the room and Jenna blushed.

"I'm sorry. I told them that you two were getting along really well. I didn't mean to overstep into your business."

"I'm sorry, too," Lori said. "I was just excited about our serious Drake coming out of his shell a little. I've lived next door to them all my life, and he's always been my hero since I was a little girl looking up to him. He's a rock. Steadfast, dependable, and will give it all for his family. And friends. But he's way too serious, and I was just excited to see the woman who's loosened him up some."

"I don't know that I do that."

Bella smiled. "Carson said both Shane and Cooper told him Drake couldn't keep his eyes off you yesterday when they all found all of you in the kitchen." Her eyes twinkled. "Are you not interested in him?"

She looked from one to the other of the four women and bit her lip as her mind reeled. "I can't honestly say no to that. I am. I mean, I'm human and female and he's…" She paused.

"Gorgeous." Jenna laughed the word and winked when Maisy gave in and nodded.

"Okay, okay, he's a walking dream man." Judging by the looks they all exchanged, she realized maybe she shouldn't have said that. "But, I'm leaving and he's not planning to marry. Did y'all not know this?"

They frowned and shared looks again.

"No, I didn't." Beth looked confused.

"I didn't either," Lori added. "And I've known him forever."

"I had no idea," Bella mused.

Jenna shook her head. "I didn't know until you told Aunt Sally Ann and me. Shane didn't either. I don't think any of his brothers know he never plans to marry. The man keeps his business to himself."

"Yes, he does," Lori added. "And he told you this? You didn't just decide this from observation?"

Lori had known him longer than anyone else in the room, so Maisy found it shocking that she or his brothers hadn't known this and he'd shared it with her.

"He told me."

"Wow." Lori's brows knitted as she crossed her arms and leaned against the counter that held the cash register and tons of paperwork for the junk shop. "I'm floored. I just always thought the right woman hadn't come along. I just don't get it."

She now knew it was strong emotions attached to the loss of his mother and the pain they'd all suffered. But considering none of them even knew he hadn't wanted to marry, she was awed again that he'd revealed this pain to her. He'd really opened up to her. She couldn't betray the trust he'd put in her.

"I'm wondering if it has something to do with losing their mom?" Jenna tapped her fingers on the counter. "He was oldest. I know it affected Shane."

"That could be it," Lori said. "I was young so I don't remember their mother but I know as we all grew up, there was a hole in their lives. I had one in mine too since my mother left me when I was two. Thank goodness for my dad and for Marcus. Even so, losing a parent does affect you. The scars run deep. And I think everyone reacts in their own way. It's also not easy losing a parent as an adult. I miss my dad every day."

It was easy to tell that Lori got it and this was why. She'd suffered a loss too. The others were quiet, and she wondered whether they understood as well. Still, she couldn't tell them what Drake had confided in her. And she remained quiet about losing her dad.

She needed to change the subject. "So, what are you doing for Libby?"

"Giving her a wedding shower tonight. We've all raced out and bought something special for her. We would love for you to join us. We've got a limousine coming and we're going for manicures and pedicures and dinner. Bella is a whiz and the minute we came up with the idea, she made some calls and we're set. We leave at five. I was going to call you but you beat me to it."

Their inclusion of her touched her. She was such a loner in so many ways, having isolated herself from making real connections with people by always moving on. It felt nice. "Sure. I would love to celebrate with all of you and Libby."

"Wonderful," Bella said. "Now we just have to

alert Libby that she's coming with us. I'll call Vance and fill him in so he can let go of her for the evening. That cowboy is so in love he's going to have a hard time doing that."

"True, but I think his brothers have something planned for him too," Beth added, with a knowing smile.

Maisy relaxed at last, which was what she needed. Being pampered a little over the evening was looking magical. And the thought of hanging out with this group of women was just what she needed.

CHAPTER ELEVEN

Drake relaxed against the banister of Cooper and Beth's large back deck and watched Cooper turning steaks on his giant grill. They'd wanted to do something special for Vance tonight and after discussing it, had decided that considering he was on the road so much that he'd probably enjoy just hanging out and relaxing. They'd been right. He was keyed up enough about getting married that it was nice to see him relaxed and laughing with all their brothers, along with Carson and Trip.

He'd heard that Maisy had gone with the gals for

the evening. He was glad, and it dawned on him that with living out of a travel trailer and going from place to place it probably left little time to make friends. She was a mystery to him. He was so used to having his family surrounding him that he couldn't imagine loading up and driving off and not seeing them often.

What's it going to be like when she drives away and he no longer saw her?

The thought struck him like lightning.

"What's the frown for?" Shane called from the table where he was about to deal cards. "Get over here and join us, big brother."

Shane's comment kicked Drake out of his deep thoughts. The table full of brothers and friends all stared at him before they all erupted with calls for him to join the game.

"Okay, okay." He realized it would help him not think about Maisy leaving so he moved across the deck and took the chair Vance held out to him.

"Sit down and let me win some big bucks off you." Vance grinned.

"Okay, because getting married, you're going to

need all you can get," he teased, knowing he'd do his best to lose as many times as he could to Vance. Growing up, he'd done it plenty of times when playing games with his younger siblings, trying to boost their spirits.

Vance grinned. "This time you can at least pretend you're trying to win. Not like when we were kids."

Chuckles rolled around the table.

"What does that mean?"

"Aw, come on, you don't think I didn't know you let me and Lana win whenever we played any games with you?"

"You knew?"

Vance shot him an of-course-I-knew look. "Ah, yeah. But it was fun letting you keep doing it."

"We just weren't sure why you didn't let us win, ever," Cooper called from the grill. "You were merciless to me, Brice, and Shane."

"Y'all were old enough and needed to know you have to work for what you get."

"We sure learned that. Especially that you were unbeatable when you set your mind to something,"

Shane said.

"That's the honest truth." Cooper laughed. "You definitely taught me if I wanted something, I needed to strive for it."

"You did it to me too," Carson added. "I might have been the little cousin, but you were relentless in your daddy-brother mode."

That had been their not-happy name for him during their hard times when they all rebelled against his bossing them around.

Trip leaned back in his chair and hooted with laughter. "Oh wow, haven't heard that in a long time."

Everyone paused the game to laugh, grinning at him.

"Hey, I wasn't that bad."

That made them chuckle more and relax back in their chairs, clearly enjoying the night as they teased him. It felt good to be here with them. They'd come a long way through the years. He was proud of each one of them. He was just their brother, but sometimes he almost felt years older than all of them. He almost felt like their dad. Which was weird in some ways considering their dad had been there too, getting through every day, living every day for his kids while hiding his sorrow.

The late-night conversation he'd shared with his dad was still bothering him. They'd invited him to join them but he'd said bachelor parties were for the younger men. Drake wondered whether he'd declined because he was struggling.

He also didn't feel all that young. Lately, he'd been feeling over the hill—at the ripe old age of thirty-seven. *You didn't feel old kissing Maisy Love.*

True. Around Maisy, he felt a great mixture of things, one of which was very much alive.

His brothers were all laughing as Shane finished passing out cards. He looked around at his happy brothers. They were content, and it showed. The only one missing was Brice, and he was driving that cattle rig as fast as he could in order to be back in time for the wedding tomorrow. After tomorrow, it would just be him and Brice who were single. He wondered when Brice would meet the special woman in his life.

"Earth to Drake," Shane said.

Vance nudged his arm. "Your turn."

He snapped out of his thoughts. "Sorry," he grunted. He glanced at his cards and laid one down.

"Are you okay?" Trip asked.

"I am. It's just been a long day. I was up most of the night."

"Why?" Shane asked.

He hesitated. He didn't want to talk about his night. Or Maisy or his conversation with his dad.

"Hey fellas," Cooper called from the grill. "Food's done. Grab your plates and your potatoes and let's dig in while they're perfect."

Drake would have to do something nice for Cooper for saving him. "It's about time," he muttered as he stood. "I was beginning to think you were burning perfectly good steaks."

Cooper shot him a glare. "Right. You know that's not happening."

Thank goodness, his timing had been perfect. When steaks were involved, these fellas would be too busy eating to press him about why he had been in la-la land. And he'd be heading home right after the food was done. It was a great night to celebrate Vance. But he was ready to head home.

He was ready to see Maisy. But that was not happening.

Tomorrow, though. He was picking her up tomorrow. And that made him smile.

Yep, the sooner he hit the hay, the sooner he'd see her.

"Are you riding with me and Gert to the wedding?" Sally Ann asked when Maisy came into the kitchen. She'd hoped Sally Ann's guests might be distracting her but they'd all left earlier to head off for some daytime adventure, leaving Maisy to face these two after all.

Gert, moving better on her healing ankle, had already arrived and looked different than she did in her jeans and shirts she wore at the café. She and Sally Ann both had on dresses. Sally Ann's blonde hair was teased a little bigger than usual and Gert's gray curls poked out from beneath a tiny hat.

She couldn't help but smile. "Well, I was going to." She took a deep breath, knowing what was about to come. "But, Drake asked me to go with him."

She had decided after all the rumors they were fueling about her and Drake that it wouldn't be a good idea to say anything until right before he was to arrive. She'd been right in saying nothing because they both reacted instantly.

Sally Ann's mouth dropped open and her eyes grew as big as hubcaps.

"Hot dog." Gert laughed and slapped the counter. "I knew it."

"Me too," Sally Ann said, having gotten her bottom jaw up off the floor. "When did he ask you?"

Their joy was contagious and she almost couldn't be mad at them for wanting to marry her off to the most eligible bachelor of Ransom Creek. Or rather, the most unattainable bachelor of Ransom Creek.

"Okay, you two, I know what you're thinking but could you please back off just a little. I'm going with him. But that's it. We're friends...well, sort of. And he asked me, even though I should have said no because of three ladies who seem to be getting a little carried away with matchmaking and I knew would get the wrong idea." She gave them a tell-me-I'm-not-wrong look. They looked half-heartedly contrite.

"We can't help it," Sally Ann blurted. "You make that man's eyes light up. Do you know how long we've been waiting on you to get here?"

This took her by surprise. "Waiting on me?"

Gert slapped a hand to her skinny hip and her pert hat snapped to the side. "Yes. We didn't just pick you out of a crowd. You burst into his life and changed it while the sweet awful scent of skunk wafted around you." She chuckled. "But it was the light in his eyes that got our attention."

"And the sparks coming out of those eyes." Sally Ann chortled.

Maisy knew there was no stopping their hope. They cared for Drake. Her heart got a funny ache thinking about all the people he cared for and all those who cared for him. "I understand why you two and Trudy care for him like this. But, please let today be about Libby and Vance and not about Drake and me."

That got them.

"You're right," Gert said. "What are we thinking?"

"We'll do that." Sally Ann sighed. "But, I hope that will also help you relax and get to know him more."

There was a knock at the door and they all looked at one another then grins burst across their faces.

Maisy's stomach tilted and she felt breathless. "Okay, you girls wait here and I'll ease out with Drake."

Their smiles faltered, and they looked forlorn, comically so. She rolled her eyes and headed down the hall and toward the front door. She almost ran she was so ready to get out of there.

She yanked the door opened so fast that she startled Drake.

"Hi." He backed up as she hustled out the door and pulled it closed behind her. "Is something wrong?"

"Oh, nothing. Let's go. Gert and Sally Ann are in there and I think I've talked them into letting today be about Vance and Libby, but who knows? They could come charging out after us at any moment, throwing rice and playing the wedding march."

He shot a glare at the house and must have come to the same realization. "Right. Come on." He took her arm and led her to his truck. He opened the door for her and she hopped inside, finally slowing down enough to catch how good he smelled. He was trying to torture her, she decided moments later when he closed his door and trapped her inside the truck with him and that scent that teased her senses.

"So, how are you?" he asked after he had backed out of the driveway and headed out of town.

"Fine. You have a lot of people in this town who care for you. And want you married off. Did you realize this?"

He hung his wrist over the steering wheel and shot her an apologetic look. "I didn't know that until you arrived. You've set the hounds on me."

"I did not do it on purpose."

"I get that."

"And besides, it's your sparkling eyes that they say did the trick."

"What sparkling eyes?"

"The ones that happen when you look at me."

He grinned. "Is that what they say?"

"Yes, so stop it and this will pass."

"That's what I've been figuring out, though. I'm not sure I can stop it."

His eyes sparkled and her heart kur-thunked against her ribs. She glared at him. "You are very confusing."

"Yeah, tell me about it. I wasn't like that before you showed up."

"Maybe all the skunk spray changed you."

"Now you might be on to something. How's your ride coming along?"

She heaved in a big breath and then sighed. "Slow. My parts are rare and stuck in Canada. It will be a few more days. But since the wedding postponed my cooking session with Gert, that gives me time to get that done."

"Sorry about that. I know you're ready to hit the road."

"I am." Her heart tugged at the idea and she stared

out the window. *Was she ready?*

"Did you and the girls have a good time last night?"

"We had a wonderful time. Your brothers and Carson and Trip married a great group of women. Poor Libby was not expecting all the pampering that she got last night. A manicure and pedicure and delicious dinner and gifts. I don't think she'd ever had a spa treatment or even gotten gifts much. She was overwhelmed. I really like her. And she is excited to marry Vance and travel with him and be able to watch him compete."

"I'm glad it was good. Vance is just as thrilled about it all himself."

They rode in silence until the ranch entrance came into view. When he pulled into the drive, there were vehicles everywhere.

"They'd thought it would just be family but they didn't anticipate how many people wished them well. And there's Lana and Cam. They made it."

He smiled as he got out of the truck and waved at a dark-haired, pregnant woman and a tall, dark-haired cowboy. Maisy got out of the truck just as he hurried around the truck and grabbed the door and held it. They stood there looking at each other. Warmth filled her and she wanted so much to feel his arms around her.

"So that's your little sister?" Her question set them both in motion. He stepped back and she did too.

"Yes, come on and I'll introduce you." He led Maisy over to his sister and brother-in-law. "Lana, Cam—glad you two made it. Vance and Libby will be thrilled." He wrapped his sister in a bear hug and she did the same to him.

"I wouldn't miss this for anything. I'm so glad we were at the ranch here in Texas. If we had been at our horse stables and with Cam's family at Windswept Bay, we wouldn't have made it on such short notice."

"I'd have tried to get her here but that would have been hard with flights or driving," Cam added, grasping Drake's outstretched hand.

Maisy waited beside Drake as Lana smiled from Drake to her. "Are you going to introduce us?"

Drake turned to Maisy. "This is Maisy Love.

She's visiting town, and she and Libby have become friends."

She shook Lana's outstretched hand and matched Lana's warm smile with one of her own. It was easy to see the speculation in her eyes. She had seen them getting out of the same truck. "I'm just passing through. It's nice to meet you both." She included Cam and shook his hand too.

"We're glad to meet you. Any friend of Libby or Drake's is a friend of ours. And you're just passing through?"

"I am. I'm hoping to leave before the week is up." She briefly explained why she was here and why she hadn't left yet. Her arm brushed Drake's and she noted that he stood closer than he needed to be.

"You're the one Aunt Trudy told me about on our last phone call. You two tangled with a skunk."

The mention of his aunt Trudy was all Maisy needed to understand the speculation in Lana's eyes. "Yes, that's us."

Drake placed his hand at the small of her back. "We better get up to the house. We don't want to keep them waiting. And you might need to sit down, Lana."

"I might. I'm having some swelling in my legs from the baby."

"Your brother is right. Let's get your feet propped up." Cam offered her his arm; she slipped hers through his and they headed toward the house.

She and Drake followed. She was very aware of his hand on her lower back.

Several cars came up the drive, including Sally Ann's truck.

Trudy had ordered some greenery and flowers for the wedding spot beside the swing. It was simple but pretty and Maisy loved it. Vance looked handsome and Libby looked so fresh and young in a delicate white dress they'd surprised her with last night. She'd planned to wear a dress that someone had given her when she'd moved to town, thinking it would be impossible to find something at such short notice. Bella had pulled that off by making a call. Her party planning skills had come in very handy. She'd also ordered some catered food, and tables were set up with a cake and punch too.

Maisy was touched by how the family had rallied around these two loved ones to make their wish come true in a beautiful way.

What would it feel like to marry? She'd pushed the idea out of her mind so long ago that suddenly imagining it seemed odd. Especially because she knew she was wondering what it would feel like to marry Drake Presley specifically.

Her breathing wobbled at the idea. And she fought to squash the ridiculous idea. The sudden ache that radiated in her heart.

Had she fallen for him?

She closed her eyes as she felt his hand return to the small of her back and then lightly slide to cup her waist as he shifted so their sides touched. The movement was not that of a man who was not interested. Was not that of a man who just wanted to be friends. *What was it?*

What did Drake want from her? He'd stated clearly that he wasn't interested in marriage.

She stiffened. *Did he think he might be able to persuade her to have a casual relationship?*

185

The idea knocked the wind out of her, it was so disappointing to her. And she didn't even understand why the idea hurt so much, but it did. She didn't have casual sex. She just hadn't ever been able to be comfortable about doing that. And though, it was true that she'd never been tempted like she was where Drake was concerned, the very idea that he might be working his way to suggesting such a thing did not sit well with her.

"I now pronounce you husband and wife. Vance, you may kiss your bride."

She blinked hard, Vance and Libby a sudden blur as they kissed. *Why had the idea that she might only be a quick and easy conquest for Drake bring these tears to her eyes?* She was grateful that when she happened to catch Lana's eyes, she, too, had tears, along with the others. Everyone would think her tears were of happiness; they wouldn't be able to tell they were from deep sadness.

There was only one explanation for her emotion.

She had fallen in love with Drake.

CHAPTER TWELVE

Drake realized with a jolt that he'd let his hand slip from Maisy's back to her waist. The move had been a shift that had come as naturally to him as if he'd been holding her by his side all of his life. It felt right. She felt right.

He only realized what he'd done when she stiffened against him, drawing him from Vance and Libby kissing. He dropped his hand immediately and leaned slightly to whisper in her ear. "Are you all right?"

"I'm fine." She stepped away from him.

If he'd needed a sign that she hadn't welcomed his touch, he had it. The bright hint of tears in her eyes confused him. *Was that because of him or the happiness of the wedding?* He'd seen tears in all his sisters-in-law's eyes and Aunt Trudy was practically weeping with joy. But, he wasn't sure what he saw in Maisy's eyes.

As he stared at her, the preacher announced Mr. and Mrs. Vance Presley and everyone cheered and clapped. He and Maisy tore their gazes apart to focus on the bride and groom and clap for them. When he looked back at Maisy, she'd silently slipped away. He searched for her and found her standing near Gert. They were clapping and whispering at the same time. And she was not looking at him.

Served him right for overstepping boundaries. *What had he been thinking, putting a possessive hand on her hip and moving closer?* He'd been pushing it by escorting her with his hand on the small of her back.

"You sure are staring at her." His dad stepped in beside him.

Drake crossed his arms, heaving in an exasperated

breath. "I'm losing it, Dad."

Marcus gave a knowing smile. "I can commiserate with you. Karla wouldn't come to the wedding with me. She said she wished Vance and Libby the best, most wonderful life but she couldn't come. And then she teared up and shut the door in my face. I don't get it, Drake. I'm trying to figure Karla out. We had a good thing going on. I really miss her. But, what about you and Maisy? You didn't share with me the other night but I know you've got her on your mind. What are you doing about it?"

He stared hard at his dad. "Even if she would consider staying in Ransom Creek, it scares me to death to think about letting myself love someone and losing them."

His dad's gaze melted. "Son, you need to stop focusing on losing her and focus on the joy and happiness of your life together. Don't you get it? No one knows how long we have on this earth. Our days are all numbered. We each have a time to die. But you can't live your life avoiding death, instead, spend it loving the time you have with those you love. Don't deny yourself that."

His dad's words echoed through him. *Was that what he was doing?*

"Go talk to her. Really talk to her."

He met his dad's gaze. "What about you? You haven't shared important aspects of your life with Karla. Why? You love her."

His dad stiffened then his shoulders dropped. "I do."

"Then maybe it's time for you to stop denying yourself making a new life with Karla."

They stared at each other and finally his dad grasped his shoulder. "Thanks for always being my right-hand man. I'll get this figured out. And I'll talk to Karla. I promise."

Drake cocked his head toward where Maisy was standing, talking to several women, and happened to glance up and meet his gaze. Time stalled and his world tilted.

"Go." His dad tugged his arm, urging him to make a move.

"Thanks, Dad," he muttered and then headed

toward the woman he'd somehow lost his heart to.

Maisy was startled when Drake caught and held her gaze across the yard. Her world shifted and her stomach went bottomless as he started toward her.

"*That* is a man on a mission," Gert stated from beside her.

"Oh my," Trudy gasped, delight in the sound. "It sure is."

Maisy felt as if she were having an out-of-body experience as he came her way. *Oh my, the man was undeniably the most gorgeous man she'd ever seen.* Her heart throbbed, wishing he was coming to declare his love for her. *It was ridiculous. Drake Presley was not the marrying kind.* But even knowing this, she couldn't look away.

"Wow, that is a man after a woman," Sally Ann said, coming from somewhere to be near enough for Maisy to hear her words.

And then he was there, standing in front of her. He didn't hesitate as he cupped her face, his touch jolting through her. And right there in front of everyone, he leaned toward her and kissed her.

She gasped, reality hitting her. "Wh-what are you doing?" She gasped as his lips melted her knees and scorched her lips.

He pulled away, his eyes boring into hers. "Come with me. We need to talk." He took her hand and headed away from the wedding party toward the barns.

Maisy glanced over her shoulder, in shock about his actions, and saw Gert, Trudy, and Sally Ann giving her the thumbs-up sign and grinning like kids rolling around in chocolate sauce.

Drake hadn't slowed but instead increased his steps and she had to jog to keep up. His grasp was firm. "Wait," she finally said, wrapping her hand over his and trying to free herself. "Drake, what are you doing?"

He didn't stop until they were in the shadow of the stable. Once inside, he spun and trapped her between him and the barn wall. "Maisy, I can't help myself. I'm in love with you. Desperately, helplessly in love."

What? Had he said what she thought he'd just

said? "You just said you loved me."

He grinned. Really grinned. "I did. And you know what? Nothing has ever sounded more right. Nothing has ever felt more right."

She needed to sit down. This was so not what she'd been expecting. "But…you're not going to marry."

"I am if you say yes."

Her hand went to her heart. "Okay, where did Drake Presley go? Who are you?"

He dropped to his knee, his gaze as intense as she'd ever seen it. "I'm not teasing you, Maisy. I love you, and until you walked into my life, I wasn't going to marry. But I didn't understand until loving you. How do you feel about me?"

She laughed. The man had really declared his love for her and asked her to marry him and he had no idea whether she loved him or couldn't stand him. Unable to halt herself, she placed both her hands on his cheeks and stared into his green eyes. His wonderful eyes. "You have thrown me for such a loop. I love you. I can't help myself. What have you done to me?"

His face exploded into the most dynamic, gorgeous smile she'd ever seen. He wrapped his arms around her thighs and lifted her up as he stood, her continuing to hold his face with her hands. And she kissed him. His lips captured hers the instant hers touched his.

He spun in the gentle sunbeam from the doorway and she was lost. Lost in his love. In his hug and the feel of him as he slowly let her slide down to where she was standing on her tiptoes, hanging onto him with all her strength.

"I hope you're serious," she muttered. "Because I'm going to have to hurt you if you're teasing me."

He laughed and pulled away to look at her. "I'm not kidding. Just lost my mental capacity the instant you kissed me. I know we have things to work out, and you making this your home base here with me might be an adjustment for you, but I can't let you go. At least, I don't want to."

"We'll get it figured out. Right now, thank you for stopping my pain. I am not sure I would have actually been able to get in my rig and drive away. Now I don't

194

have to."

He smiled. His eyes turned dreamy, and he lowered his mouth just above hers. "How did I live without you?"

"I have no idea." She giggled, then pulled his head down and joined their lips.

EPILOGUE

"**O**kay, so everyone hush," Gert boomed on Tuesday to the diner that was filled to capacity. "We're thrilled as peach pie that all of you have come out to watch our very own Maisy Love— soon to be Maisy Presley, cook with me on her internet channel. Now, all you cowboys smile real pretty when Jenna here sweeps the crowd and everyone look like you're really enjoying the food. I don't want any sour faces because I'm hoping to get some more business coming in here with this taping. And like I said, anyone here today is getting free cobblers on the house."

"With ice cream," Cooper called out from where he sat with Beth, Shane and Jenna."

"That's right, ice cream too," Gert assured him.

"I'll smile twice as big for your cobbler and ice cream too," Brice drawled. He was sitting at a table with Drake who could not stop grinning from ear to ear as he prepared to watch Maisy get the surprise of her life. She had no idea what was about to happen.

He watched her smiling behind Gert as she made sure every detail was perfect for the show. In the few days since he'd asked her to marry him they'd spent hours talking and planning. Their careers were going to be fine together. She was strong and independent and would continue her traveling show as long as she wanted to. He would travel with her some, but had no intention of smothering her. Despite the fact that he could be very happy spending every moment of the day and night with her she was a free spirit, and he liked the idea of adapting to her lifestyle some. He planned on loosening up, though his brothers weren't believers yet he planned to shock them a bit. Their first trip was coming soon as they headed down to see her mother. Maisy wanted to at least try to mend the rift that was between them and he wanted to be by her side as she did.

As if knowing he was thinking about her, Maisy looked directly at him and smiled. He was a lucky man. Blessed that she'd found him.

"Okay," she said, pulling her eyes off of him and taking in the room. "Here we go. Let's have fun with this, shall we?"

"I think with you involved that's the only way it can go," he said, drawing her smile.

Brice leaned in across the corner of the table and said in low tones, "I told you that you were going to fall hard, big brother."

"Yep, you were right. You're next you know," Drake leveled laughing eyes on him.

Brice looked unimpressed. "Not till I'm ready. I've got plans of my own. I'll let all of you have your fun and I'll have mine."

"I'll do that but I'm telling you when love slams into you it takes your breath away and turns your well-

198

planned out world upside down."

"Right, but only if you're willing. And you were willing."

Drake grinned again at Maisy who had started the show and was interviewing one proud and beaming Gert Goodnight. "I might not have been willing at first but I soon threw in the towel and dove in the deep end, more than willing."

Brice said something else, but he wasn't listening, he was lost in watching Maisy doing what she loved. And waiting for the surprise to walk in.

As if on cue the door opened, and a guy walked inside followed by a camera man. Maisy saw him the moment he walked through the door and she froze. Her pretty mouth fell open as her words trailed off.

"Maisy Love, I presume," Tac Storm said with a big grin that matched the one on Gert's face. Gert had known the show was going to be interrupted by the famous cooking show host.

"Yes, yes that's me," Maisy said after Gert elbowed her in the rib. "You're Tac Storm," she half laughed as if everyone didn't already know that.

Truth was, Drake hadn't known until Gert told him about the man and the show and he'd checked it out.

"That's me, and I'm making a few stops for the big competitor reveal and Ms. Goodnight was kind enough to let us bust in on your show with a little surprise for you."

Maisy's expression went from shocked to more shocked as she looked from Tac to Gert. "What?"

The room was quiet as everyone was taking in the scene.

Gert grinned. "I'll let Tac spill the beans."

"You've been selected to do your thing and compete on my show against four other top cooks in the country. We loved your video you sent in and think our viewers will get a kick out of watching you in action. What do you say, Maisy Love, are you in?"

Maisy's eyes glistened and shot straight to Drake. He grinned at her and his heart filled up even more with love for her. "Well, I didn't think I'd ever see you at a loss for words," he said and chuckled. "Say yes."

She laughed. "Yes, I'd love to and Drake is right, you made me speechless."

Tac Storm grinned. "Long as you aren't speechless come competition time that's fine with me. Now, if you don't mind, how's about letting me get in on this show you and the pretty little Ms. Goodnight have going on?"

Maisy got her wings beneath her in that moment. "Please do. That way I can mark off the number two item on my bucket list."

Tac looked offended. "Number two? Hey, now, I kind of like being number one on people's list."

Her smile widened and her eyes twinkled as they landed on Drake. "Sorry, but marrying that cowboy right there is number one on my list."

Drake loved this woman. Loved her with every breath of his being. However, he was not expecting the camera man to turn the camera on him and Tac to place his hands on his hips and stare at him.

"Well, then if that's the case, only thing I can

think of to help this show be even better is if we have the lucky cowboy help us cook. What do you say, Maisy?"

She laughed as did the entire café. "I think that would be amazing," she said and motioned for him to stand up.

Drake frowned at the camera, no words. Tac was laughing too, obviously doing off-the-cuff things was part of his show.

"Go on, big brother, get on up there," Brice urged. "Cowboy up," he chuckled. "You can do it."

He glared at Brice who was about to fall out of his chair with glee and then Maisy was standing beside him. "Cook with me, Drake," she said and took his hand.

He looked down into her eyes and sighed. "Darlin', lead the way. I'm all yours."

"Good, because I'm all yours too." And then, for the whole world to see as the cameras rolled, Maisy Love wrapped her arms around his neck and kissed him weak-kneed.

With his brothers whooping in the background he heard Brice's deep drawl. "Well, big brother, I'd say maybe you are loosening up."

No maybes about it—with Maisy in his life loosening up was the only way.

And he was lovin' every minute of it.

Excerpt from

BRICE: NOT QUITE LOOKING FOR A FAMILY

Cowboys of Ransom Creek, Book Seven

CHAPTER ONE

Brice Presley had missed out on his brother's quick wedding because he'd been delivering cattle when Vance had had a window of opportunity to rush home, marry Libby over the weekend, and then head back out for his next rodeo. He hated missing the wedding, but he understood why Vance would want to have Libby on the road with him and that he'd had to squeeze the impromptu wedding in when he could.

Vance was making another attempt at winning the National Finals Rodeo Championship and he couldn't stand not having the love of his life with him as he competed, therefore he'd fixed it by marrying her on a day that Brice happened to be out of town delivering cattle. Brice had talked to Vance by phone right after the ceremony and congratulated him and he'd noted that Vance sounded content...like he could conquer the world now.

Content was a word that Brice was seeing all his brothers experiencing and now that Drake was also engaged, he felt a bit melancholy. Life was changing around him and he felt a little like it was moving on without him.

He didn't like the feeling. But as he led a mustang out to the round pen to work, he caught sight of his dad trudging from the barn. Marcus paused to look at the sun then headed toward Brice. Lately, his dad hadn't been himself and they were all worried about him. Drake had revealed to them that their dad's girlfriend, Karla, had broken up with him. This had left Marcus Presley in a daze. It was the only word Brice could come up with that rightly described the way he seemed these days.

"Hey, Dad?" Brice called. "Are you looking for me?"

"I am. I just got a call from Frank Leonard. He said his new renter is moving in tomorrow and he asked if one of you boys would go down and make sure water and electricity is turned on and running right. He had some plumbing issues and had a company go out and fix it but he'd just like to make sure that everything is on and in good working order. You're the only one around, so if you don't mind?"

He didn't mind. Frank was a nearby rancher who had leased his land to them when he and his wife had decided to semi-retire, lease out their home, and do some traveling. To Brice, this was an odd thing for a rancher to do, but he figured if that was what he wanted, then more power to him. But finding a renter for the big house out here in Ransom Creek had proved to be harder than expected.

"He finally found someone to rent the place?"

"Yes, a single woman with two kids."

"Really? And she's moving into that big house?"

"I guess so. Not sure what she does that would have her moving out here or want that big place."

Brice glanced at his horse. "Let me put this one back in its pen and I'll head over there."

"Thanks." Marcus turned and started back toward the house.

"Dad, how are you doing? Have you talked to Karla lately?"

He turned back, his gaze a little lost, and even a little angry. "No. I tried but she asked me not to come around anymore."

He hated seeing his dad looking down. Before Karla had come into his life, he'd been fine—maybe not as fine as they'd thought but at least he'd seemed happy and very involved with the ranch, like they all were. But then he'd had the unexpected heart attack and met Karla at the hospital when she'd been his nurse. There had been a change in him after that. He'd actually started dating and had been giving more of his ranch duties to him and his brothers. They'd all been happy to see him finally taking some time for himself and they'd been hopeful that maybe marriage would be in the future for them. And then Karla had suddenly ended their relationship. And his dad hadn't understood why.

He believed she wanted marriage but his dad was dragging his feet. To some extent Brice understood this, he wasn't sure he ever wanted the complications that came from a serious relationship. He'd witnessed the hurt and pain his father had gone through after their mother died giving birth to his little sister, Lana. Watched his dad work himself silly through the years taking care of them and the ranch. And Brice still felt like there was a hole in his heart where his mother was missing. However, he had also witnessed the change in his dad when Karla came into his life and it had given them all a new hope that love could bloom again for his dad.

"Thought she might have changed her mind," he said. "Are you going to be okay?"

"I'll be okay. Don't worry about me. Thanks for taking care of this."

"Any time." Brice led the horse back into the

stable and as he returned him to his stall the other horses came to look over their gates, thinking one of them was up next on the morning exercise routine. "Sorry, fellas. I'll be back."

Brice had been delivering the Presley brand cattle all over the country and also oversaw the reproduction phase of their business on the days he wasn't on the road. Right now, things in that department were timed out as they'd already done in vitro on their cows and were now waiting for the babies to be birthed in January and February. That gave Brice time to devote to breaking a few of the wild mustangs that the ranch rescued then rehabilitated so they could be adopted out. He enjoyed the process and it was rewarding when they had a family or another ranch adopt a mustang.

A few minutes later, with an old Clint Black tune playing on the radio, he pulled into the drive of the neighbor's ranch. It was down the road and on the other side from their ranch. The house sat off the paved road a piece and he drove at a fast pace down the red dirt drive. It was hot and dry and the dirt plumed behind him as if he were being chased by a dust storm.

This land was pretty, much like their own, with rolling pastureland dotted by huge ancient oak trees and ponds that allowed the cattle to drink from or to cool off in during the hot Texas summers. Brice had toyed with the idea of offering to buy it from the Leonards so that he would have his own place. When he'd hoped his dad and Karla might eventually get married, he'd realized he wouldn't want to remain in their ranch house with the newlyweds. Now, though that possibility seemed to have come to a halt, he still thought about his own place. It was time. Then too, he loved being involved in the ranch with his family but lately he'd been feeling the desire to build something of his own, on the side while still being involved with the family ranch.

He represented the ranch when he pulled up and delivered the stock to the buyers but being on the road so much was starting to bug him. He'd dealt with missing Vance's wedding, but it still bothered him that he'd been at the opposite end of Texas when his little brother had surprised them with a quick wedding. As he crossed the Leonard ranchland his discontent suddenly rose to a new level. They could hire drivers, he'd just done it because he'd wanted to...because being confined to one spot had always suffocated him to some extent in a way he didn't completely understand, but something was changing in him.

He would talk to Drake about it and he'd get a plan of action lined up that began with making an offer on this ranch. This new woman coming to the Leonard's ranch was a kink in his plan, but she was a renter and there were other places to rent.

Pulling his truck to a stop he noticed a ranch truck parked near the barn. He'd thought Mr. Leonard had sold all of his ranch trucks and trailers. Hopping from his truck, he glanced around but spotted no one. Figuring he must have been wrong about the rancher's trucks, Brice strode up the sidewalk. His spurs jangled as he walked on the concrete, the soft purr of the spur the only sound on the dry afternoon. It was a lonesome sound in the secluded area. This place needed a keeper. He should have already offered to buy it. Someone was going to make the offer before he had a chance and that would serve him right for dragging his boots.

He reached for the hidden key, normally on the edge of the doorframe, but it wasn't there. He frowned, then remembered the plumber had been there the day before. He tried the door and it opened. He wasn't happy that the plumber had left the place unlocked. Not that the key was hidden all that well, but still, if you hired someone to do a job, they should lock up when they left.

The place was an open concept with wood floors and solid beams spanning the vaulted ceiling. It had a nice kitchen and the furnishings were rustic Texas décor. It was a comfortable place. A great place to raise a family…he was just now planning on buying his own place as a man in his thirties but having a family—he was not ready for that step. And he might never be.

Having only himself to worry about—and his dad and siblings was different than having a wife and kids of his own to worry over.

Still, the idea splintered through his mind like a whip crack splitting the air. Ignoring it, he moved to the sink and turned on the water. It seemed fine. He headed to the upstairs bedroom to check how the toilets were flushing. As he entered one of the smaller guest bedrooms the sound of running water had him hurrying. Had the plumber not only left the front door unlocked but also left the shower running? He hoped he hadn't left the tub stopper in.

He pushed open the partly closed door and was instantly enveloped in warm steam. The mirror was fogged up. "What the heck?" he muttered, the instant a blood-curdling scream filled the small room, sounding like a wild mountain lion on attack.

He stumbled back and slammed into the bathroom counter at the same time the shower curtain was yanked down and clutched around a soapy-haired woman who only screamed louder at the sight of him. *Who—what?*

"Who are you?" she demanded, finding her voice and shutting off the scream before he could get out any words. She glared at him from behind the protection of the horse-covered shower curtain. Blonde hair full of white suds clung to her wet skin and her blue eyes shot blue blazes at him.

He was speechless, completely blank as he stared.

"*What* are you doing here?" she demanded again, her voice strong as she reached for a back scrubber dangling from where it hung on a hook beneath the pelting shower nozzle. She held it like a sword while she kept a death grip on the plastic shower curtain and tried to deal with the awkward shower rod that was now caught half in the curtain hooks and half out. She was dealing with a lot but definitely ready to beat him to death with anything she could.

Wow. She was fierce.

As the thought slammed into him, his brain clicked in. He held out his hands. "Calm down. I'm not here to hurt you. Who are you and what are you doing here? I'm here to work…" His brain stalled looking at her. Why was he here? "…on the plumbing." Yeah, that was it. Plumbing…had brought him here, and looking at the suds covered beauty he'd never been so thankful for leaky pipes in all of his life.

Who was she?

Tara Quinn hid her fear as she forced strength and confidence into her voice to appear unafraid. Not that the back scrubber with its loofah-sponged end was going to protect her if this lean, muscled, broad-shouldered cowboy decided to come at her. But she was a fighter. The good Lord had put an over-abundance of fight in her, maybe because he'd known she was going to need every ounce of it this last year. *This cowboy was about to find out he'd tangled with the wrong woman.* She clung to the shower curtain and tried to ignore the fact that the shower rod, half dangling from the hooks of the shower curtain, might be a better weapon than the loofa. Getting it untangled might be a problem, though. Thankfully, she knew how to use her knees and elbows too.

She pointed the back scrubber at him. "I'm renting this place. I didn't call a plumber."

"Awe, you're the renter." He relaxed at her words. "You aren't supposed to be here until tomorrow."

216

"How did you know that?"

"Mr. Leonard told me. Well, actually my dad told me because he's the one who Mr. Leonard called and asked if me or one of my brothers could come check on a water issue." The cowboy leaned against the counter and crossed his arms and grinned charmingly. "I wasn't expecting to find you in the shower when he sent me over here."

Her adrenaline was slowing and her heart calming down, she was more and more aware of the pelting of the water from the shower and the soap sliding down her face and getting near her eyes as she stared at the cowboy. He was absolutely too comfortable as he settled against the counter and grinned at her.

She frowned. "I can assure you when I got into this shower, I wasn't expecting to be intruded upon by the likes of you. Now, if it's not inconveniencing you too much to get up from your relaxed position sitting on my counter, I'd like to get dressed."

The guy was unbelievable—she was calling her landlord the minute she was dressed.

"Sorry." He shot up from the counter and at least

looked repentant. "You're right. I'm just still in shock, and my knees are a little weak. That back scrubber almost gave me a heart attack."

"Funny. Now leave."

Chuckling, he headed out the door. "I'll wait for you in the kitchen," he called as he disappeared from sight.

"The nerve—who was this guy anyway?" she growled, realizing he hadn't said his name, just that the landlord had sent him. Her blood still boiling, she stepped from the shower and tripped on the curtain rod. She flew forward and just barely managed not to hit the wooden floor as she grabbed the countertop to keep from falling. Steadying herself she reached for the door and slammed it shut then snapped the lock into place. Her blood was boiling as she took a breath and tried to calm down. Of course, soap dripped into her eyes in that instant and the stinging drove her back toward the shower for a quick rinse. Squinting, because her eyes were burning she moved quickly, too quickly stepping onto the slippery porcelain bathtub—

"No," she gasped, clawing for something to stop

her fall. But all she grabbed was air as her feet slid sideways and down she went.

Her hip hit first, then her back, and then her temple.

"Owe…" she yelped, as she stared up at the white ceiling and saw stars before the room dimmed.

"Are you okay in there?" the cowboy demanded loudly through the door. He shook it. "Did you fall?"

She closed her eyes. *Of course he'd heard her.* She was very thankful she'd locked the door as she envisioned him busting into the bathroom to find her in nothing but her birthday suit sprawled in the tub.

"Answer me, if you can."

He was so irritating. "I'm fine." Her voice came out much weaker than the forceful way she'd hoped. "Go awayyy."

"You don't sound fine." He jiggled the door again.

Panic rocketed through the fog. "Don't come in," she barked, making her building headache pound. She grabbed the sides of the tub—which wasn't hard considering one arm was already draped over it—and then she slid to a sitting position. She shook her head to clear it but only succeeded in making her head hurt worse and the room to spin faster. She tried to ignore the pain and the spin, and grabbed for the towel that dangled off the back of the toilet. She missed. She grunted and tried again, and managed to snag the corner of it.

"Seriously, did you fall?"

She dragged the towel to her only then realizing that the shower water was still pelting her. She leaned forward and got the lever turned off then pulled the soaking towel over her. It gave her a semblance of security just in case the cowboy Neanderthal came busting through the door to rescue her.

"If you don't answer me, I'm coming in."

She had forgotten to answer him. "I'm fine," she forced the words through clenched teeth.

"You do not sound fine. You did fall, didn't you? Did you hit your head?"

She had to take a moment to think about that... "Yes, I did," she muttered, feeling weaker. *Why hadn't she remembered that?*

"That does it. If you can't open the door, I'm

busting it down."

Suddenly there was a wood splintering crash at the door. Clutching the towel over her body she screamed. He must have thrown his weight against the door but thankfully it held.

"Don't come through that door," she yelped, managing to sit up fully. "I'm getting out. Stop."

"What if you fall again?"

She gritted her teeth. "I won't." She hoped. "Just wait." She eased to stand up but felt very wobbly as she held onto the tub's edge while she stepped out and onto the rug.

She grabbed a dry towel from where it hung on the towel rack above the toilet and wrapped it around her body then secured the tail, tucking it tightly above her left breast. She leaned against the wall as dizziness swamped her. She must have groaned.

"You still don't sound good. I'm coming in. Are you covered?"

"I am, but wait a moment and I'll get to the door. I'm just dizzy."

She kept her back to the wall and sidestepped

toward the door, sliding along the wall. Thankfully, it wasn't a huge bathroom, not like the master bath, which was big enough for three of these bathrooms to fit inside. The door would have been a long way away from the shower if she'd hurt herself in there. Relief and trepidation filled her at the same time as she made it to the door and unlocked it.

Why hadn't she brought her clothes into the bathroom? she wondered, then remembered that there was not supposed to be anyone in the house, so she'd left them in the bedroom.

She hoped she didn't pass out or all modesty would be lost to her.

The door opened and the cowboy stuck his head inside. The instant his gaze met hers, his eyes widened and he moved inside.

"That's not good," he said, his eyes wide with alarm.

"What?" she asked, reminding herself that if he hadn't barged in on her in the first place, she never would have slipped and hit her head.

He moved toward her and she stepped back too

quickly, causing the room to spin. Instantly, she wobbled and her knees seemed to melt beneath her. She grabbed for anything to keep her from falling and this time she grabbed his shirt—just as she was swept into the safety of powerful arms and a hard chest.

"Hold on."

Worry slammed into Brice as he scooped the pretty blonde into his arms. She had less suds in her hair and on her face now. The shower that he'd heard stop running after he'd heard her fall must have washed them away before she got the water turned off. She blinked up at him with dazed eyes and his pulse sped up more than the hundred miles an hour it was already doing. The instant he'd heard the crash in the bathroom he'd been scared something bad had happened. The black-and-blue bump forming above her left eye was bad but he worried about what he couldn't see behind those dazed eyes of hers.

"The room is spinning," she moaned.

"You have a bump the size of Texas on your

forehead." He didn't hesitate as he turned and headed toward the bedroom as she struggled with the towel. He looked straight ahead, not wanting to add to her discomfort as she clutched the towel about her.

"That big?" she groaned, stiffening in his arms, as they entered the bedroom. "What are you doing? Put me down. And don't look at me."

"I'm not going to look at you and I am putting you down. Just be still and hold on to your towel. You'll be fine." Her being aware that she needed the towel at least told him she wasn't as dazed as he'd thought. He strode to the bed and placed her on it, then pulled the cover across her. He stepped back and jammed his hands to his hips and studied that bump. "That thing is growing. Is your head feeling like it's about to split open?"

She nodded.

"You look pale too. Maybe I better take you to the clinic."

"No, I'm fine. I'm dazed, true enough, but after some pain meds I'll be fine. Now, please, could you just go? You've caused enough problems."

She was right. "And that's why I'm not going to leave you here alone after you slammed your head on a porcelain bathtub."

"I'm not going to the hospital."

He pulled his phone from his pocket and dialed the best person he knew to ask about the situation: Karla, his dad's girlfriend. Ex-girlfriend. She was a nurse and maybe she could talk sense into the woman.

"Do not call the ambulance," his injured neighbor snapped then rubbed her forehead and lay back on the pillows, clearly hurting.

"I'm calling a nurse. Karla," he said the moment she answered. "This is Brice."

"Brice," Karla said, pleasure radiating in her voice.

He'd always thought of her voice as a reassuring mixture of strength and kindness that was soothing to her patients at the hospital. He hated that she and his dad's relationship was not working out. He'd hoped that his father might have finally found someone he could love and move on from the tragic past, the death of his wife. Brice and all of his siblings had been hoping Karla was the woman who could win their dad's heart. But something was wrong between them and it wasn't looking good for them right now.

"I have an emergency—"

"Is it your dad?" she asked, her voice tight.

Brice heard the fear in her words and hated that he'd scared her. "No, it's a woman. She hit her head in the shower and is looking dazed. There is a large bump forming on her forehead. I've dealt with cowboys with kicks to the head from cows and horses, but this is a woman." He was sure she could hear the fear in his voice now, as he glanced at the woman. She glared at him, defiant even though he knew her head had to be hurting.

Ice.

The thought popped into his brain and he spun and headed immediately to the kitchen. Of course he needed ice.

"Okay, put some ice on the swelling," she said, as if reading his mind.

"On my way. The bump is above her left eye and she's not happy I'm calling for help. She says she's fine. But she looks stunned. I'm thinking I should call the ambulance."

"No. Not yet. There is no need to panic. If she won't go with the ambulance, there is no need calling them. Put the ice on the swelling and watch her eyes. And don't let her go to sleep for more than two hours at a time."

"But...I just came here to check the water." He didn't even know her name and he could tell she was not going to be happy to have a total stranger dictating her day to her.

"If there isn't anyone else around, you need to watch her."

"She's not going to like that." He yanked open the freezer and saw there was plenty of ice in the container. He started opening drawers, looking for a dishcloth or plastic bag.

"Well, you wouldn't be the first nurse not to get a warm reception by a patient."

"This is awkward. I thought if you happened to be in the neighborhood, it would sure be helpful if you could swing by."

There was a pause. "I'm not. You can do this."

"Okay, it was worth a shot. I'll call one of the girls," he said, now eager to call one of his brothers' wives. He needed a female out here and he needed her yesterday. He should have known Karla wasn't in town. Since she'd gotten mad at his dad, she'd stopped coming around—a big shame. But because she was a nurse, she'd been his first call.

"Let me know how it turns out." She finished with symptoms to watch for that would mean to get her to a hospital even if she didn't want to go, like passing out. He hoped she didn't pass out or get worse. At least not before she could get her clothes on.

"I will. Thanks. And, Karla, I'm real sorry things didn't work out between you and Dad."

"Me too. Talk later."

He didn't hesitate as he ended the call but instantly called Beth, thinking she was his best bet on being home and the closest to them considering her and Cooper's place was next to the ranch.

"Come on, pick up," he muttered as he listened to the ringtones.

"Hello."

"Beth," he blurted the instant he heard her voice. "I need you over here at Frank Leonard's place. Can you get here in a few seconds? It's an emergency."

"Sure. What's wrong?" she asked, and he could hear the door slam and her jogging down the wooden steps from their deck.

He told her what had happened as she got in her truck. "Gottcha. I'll be there as soon as I can be." The sound of the engine roaring to life sent relief through him.

He might not be ready to put down roots and get married, but he was especially glad his brothers had been. He loved his new sisters-in-law. All of them.

He hadn't had any idea one of them would come to his rescue like Beth was doing right now. He just hoped she got here soon.

More Books in the Series

Cowboys of Ransom Creek
Trip: Her Cowboy Hero (Book 1)
Carson: The Cowboy's Bride for Hire (Book 2)
Cooper: Charmed by the Cowboy (Book 3)
Shane: The Cowboy's Junk-Store Princess (Book 4)
Vance: Her Second-Chance Cowboy (Book 5)
Drake: The Cowboy and Maisy Love (Book 6)
Brice: Not Quite Looking for a Family (Book 7)

Check out Debra's Other Series
Star Gazer Inn of Corpus Christi Bay
Cowboys of Dew Drop, Texas
Sunset Bay Romance
Texas Brides & Bachelors
New Horizon Ranch Series
Turner Creek Ranch Series
Texas Matchmaker Series
Windswept Bay Series

About the Author

Debra Clopton is a USA Today bestselling & International bestselling author who has sold over 3.5 million books. She has published over 81 books under her name and her pen name of Hope Moore.

Under both names she writes clean & wholesome and inspirational, small town romances, especially with cowboys but also loves to sweep readers away with romances set on beautiful beaches surrounded by topaz water and romantic sunsets.

Her books now sell worldwide and are regulars on the Bestseller list in the United States and around the world. Debra is a multiple award-winning author, but of all her awards, it is her reader's praise she values most. If she can make someone smile and forget their worries for a few hours (or days when binge reading one of her series) then she's done her job and her heart is happy. She really loves hearing she kept a reader from doing the dishes or sleeping!

A sixth-generation Texan, Debra lives on a ranch in Texas with her husband surrounded by cattle, deer, very busy squirrels and hole digging wild hogs. She enjoys traveling and spending time with her family.

Visit Debra's website and sign up for her newsletter
for updates at: www.debraclopton.com

Check out her Facebook at:
www.facebook.com/debra.clopton.5

Follow her on Instagram at: debraclopton_author

or contact her at debraclopton@ymail.com

Printed in Great Britain
by Amazon

22239668R00136